What Ever Happened to Mr. MAJIC?

By
Rod Pennington
&
Jeffery A. Martin

Integration Press
Jackson, Wyoming

What Ever Happened to Mr. MAJIC?

Copyright © 2019 by Rod Pennington

The art for the cover came from an original oil by Lisa Hadley of Jackson Hole, Wyoming titled "Over the Hills"

ISBN 13: 978-1-57242-165-3 Trade Paper
ISBN 13: 978-1-57242-170-7 Ebook

Library of Congress Control Number: 2018913227

Integration Press
P.O. Box 8906
Jackson, Wyoming 83002

What Ever Happened to Mr. MAJIC?

By
Rod Pennington
&
Jeffery A. Martin

CHAPTER ONE

"WHAT DO YOU MEAN, you're not my father?"

"That's not what I said, Gracie." The man I had always called Dad shifted his weight uncomfortably and, for the first time that I could remember in my entire life, had trouble making eye contact with me. "Of course I'm your father. I'm just not your biological father."

I blinked a few times, then looked down at the open grave where the simple wooden coffin was resting. The two handfuls of dirt my sister and I had tossed on it moments earlier were still visible.

"Really? You're telling me this now?"

Dad started to say something, then thought better of it and held his peace. That was so like him. He was never a big talker when things were going well and got even more laconic when things got rough. I just looked at him and shook my head. The smart money would bet he had wanted to tell me sooner, maybe much sooner, but the lady in the box at my feet had said no.

Don Maxwell — AKA Dad — whose wardrobe choice tended more toward denim and flannel than worsted, had added a few pounds since the last time he had worn a suit and tie. He'd had to pull and stretch the collar of the dress shirt he had found in the back of his closet to get the top button to reach its hole. From the moment he put it on, it had been chafing his neck. With most of the well-wishers already heading back to their cars, he undid the top button and loosened the Jerry Garcia tie I had given him as a gag gift for Christmas a few years back.

Shaking my head again, I tried to make sense of all of this, but I kept coming up empty. I nodded in the direction of my younger sister, Sunny, whose fair skin and blonde hair were in stark contrast to the black dress she was wearing. She was sitting on one of the graveside folding chairs with an ethereal, almost trancelike, expression on her face. Next to her, in a well-tailored suit over a custom-made shirt topped off by a handmade silk tie, was her boyfriend, Willie Hanson. Hanson had been in my graduating class in high school, and I remembered him as being kind of a weird computer nerd who, like me, kept mostly to himself, and was a wicked keyboard player. He was also my top competition for valedictorian. The last I had heard of him, he had dropped out of Stanford to try his hand at a Silicon Valley startup. I was a bit surprised to see him back in the Eastern Time Zone.

"I assume Sunny is all yours." His eyes locked on mine. Don Maxwell gritted his teeth and muttered, "Yes."

"Does she know about me?"

"I can't speak for your mother, but I never told her," Don Maxwell answered.

Out of the corner of my eye, I saw a man I had never seen before heading toward us. He was small and probably closer to sixty than forty. His nose was too big, his chin too small, and his eyes too close together for him to ever have been considered handsome by any measure. He paused, looked around, then zeroed in on me and began walking purposefully in my direction.

"Who's that?"

Don Maxwell turned, and when he saw the approaching man, his shoulders slumped; he shook his head and sighed. Before he could formulate a response, the man arrived next to the grave site, and his eyes locked on me.

"Ms. Grace Bliss Maxwell?" the man said in a voice that was deeper than expected considering his diminutive size.

I nodded.

"My condolences for your loss. I am Wilson Prentice, attorney-at-law." The lawyer pulled a number 10 envelope out of the interior pocket of his ill-fitting suit jacket that hung badly on his shoulders. He had the unhealthy look of someone who had lost a lot of weight in a short amount of time. "Your mother instructed me to give you this after her death."

Don Maxwell was seething and now it was his turn to think *couldn't this have waited until tomorrow?* Then it dawned on me. Don knew the lawyer might show up at any moment, and he wasn't being cruel — he was being kind. He didn't want me to hear this news from a stranger.

Reluctantly I accepted the envelope. "What is this?"

"My instructions were to deliver this to you unopened." Prentice bowed slightly and handed me one of his business cards. "Again, my condolences for your loss." Without another word, he turned and headed back in the direction of his car.

Examining the envelope, I immediately recognized the handwriting. On the outside of the envelope was written a single word.

Grace.

The thin, precise script bordered on calligraphy. My entire life I had seen it on everything from school permission slips to grocery lists.

With trembling hands, I carefully tore open the envelope.

> *Grace:*
>
> *By now I assume Don has told you he is not your biological father. Please do not be angry with him for not telling you sooner; that was entirely my decision. I had always meant to tell you, but when I got sick, time ran out.*
>
> *To his great credit, when I came home pregnant with you, Don took me back, made an honest woman of me, and claimed you as his own.*
>
> *He has loved you from the day you were born more than you'll ever imagine.*
>
> *Trust him and listen to him. But most importantly, love him. More than anyone in your life, he has earned it.*
>
> *You are now a full-grown woman, and it is only fair that you know the truth. Your biological father is a man known as Simon Alphonse Peterson.*
>
> *You also need to know, having you back in my life these last few months was a blessing. I can only hope you find peace and happiness.*
>
> *Peace Love & Joy Always,*
> *Mom*

As I reread the cryptic note, Willie Hanson kissed my sister on the forehead and softly said, "I'll see you at the wake."

Sunny forced a weak smile and gave his arm a squeeze. "Okay." Her eyes locked on the departing lawyer, and she wandered over and joined the conversation. "What's going on? Who was that?"

I looked at Don for guidance.

With an odd expression on his face, he just shrugged. "Your call, Gracie."

Drawing in a deep breath, then releasing it with a snort, I said, "What the hell," and handed Sunny the letter.

She read the note, blinked a few times, shook her head like she was clearing it of cobwebs, then reread it more slowly. "Huh?" she said as she handed it back to me.

"Huh? That's all you've got?" I said incredulously.

"What? You've said it yourself a thousand times. We were always so different when we were growing up, it was hard to believe we were sisters."

I shook my head again and turned my attention back to Don Maxwell. "Who is Simon Alphonse Peterson?"

He lowered his eyes. Obviously this was a painful topic for him, but, like always, it wasn't going to stop him from toughing his way through it. He glanced down at the open grave. "It's a long story, and this isn't the time or the place. We need to get to the wake. After we get past that, I'll tell both of you everything I know."

CHAPTER TWO

S UNNY'S FINGERS DANCED across the screen of her iPhone as she sat next to me in the back of the limo the funeral home had provided. Don, formerly known as Dad, knew the driver and had opted to sit up front; but I suspected what he really wanted to do was give Sunny and me some space to discuss Mom's little final parting shot to her estranged eldest daughter. My body was numb as I stared aimlessly out the window, but my eyes couldn't focus, and my mind was racing. Losing Mom was expected and, considering the pain she was in toward the end, was in some ways a blessing. I had had time to prepare myself for it, had already pretty much moved through the five stages of grief, and had, more or less, embraced acceptance. The news of my newly discovered biological father was another matter entirely. It was like a well-placed body blow I hadn't seen coming. While it hadn't knocked me to my knees, it had left me gasping and stunned.

How could my parents have kept this from me for over twenty-three years?

While Mom and I were never that close, once I learned her prognosis, I called her every day, which had given her ample opportunity to tell me this news herself, but she didn't. Why not? Sure, Mom and I saw the world so differently, it was always hard for us to communicate with each other. It was almost like we spoke different languages. But why not tell me this when she had the chance instead of letting me find out the way I did? With Mom you could never tell. It was not in her nature to be hurtful or spiteful, so there had to be another reason she didn't share this important news. Maybe she was afraid of how I would react and thought I would abandon her. Maybe she just didn't want to go out on a sour note. Maybe she had one of her elaborate plans in motion

— which I'd always found so painfully annoying while growing up — to try to influence me without actually coming right out and telling me what to do. Hard to say.

One thing was clear from all of our chats: Mom didn't want me to experience any survivor's guilt because of our strained relationship. Whenever I would get maudlin or weepy at the missed opportunity to spend our lives together, she would buck me up. She always kept our conversations light and breezy, and we only reminisced about the good times and ignored the bad.

Don, on the other hand? His keeping the secret was no mystery at all. He was as uncomplicated and straightforward as a person could possibly be. More often than not, he and I were on the same wavelength my entire life, and he never gave me the slightest reason to doubt he was my father. I was sure he'd wanted to tell me, but I was also equally sure that Mom, for her own reasons, had vetoed it. What baffled me was why she'd done so.

"Huh," Sunny said as she rapidly swiped the screen of her phone.

"Is that the only word in your vocabulary today?" I asked in an annoyed tone as the blur of the landscape whizzed past.

While we were only twenty months apart in age and raised by the same parents and in the same house, it had always been hard to understand how my sister and I could possibly be so different. Not so much anymore, with this interesting twist in the branch of the family tree coming to light.

Sunny's personality and appearance perfectly matched her name, and she was a dead ringer for our mom. A solid three inches taller than me, Sunny had an alabaster complexion and could get a sunburn walking between the house and her car. Our mother used to say Sunny was born in a state of total enlightenment and that somehow she had managed to not screw it up. Whatever the hell that meant. Like Mom, Sunny lived in the moment, and nothing ever seemed to bother her. Her entire life, Sunny always blazed her own trail and never followed the crowd, but the crowd had a persistent habit of following her. Being a self-contained and independent free spirit, she fully embraced and thrived on the long leash Mom gave us while we were growing up.

On the other extreme, where Sunny was long and lean, I was more compact with a much darker complexion and tended to be introspective and moody. I looked absolutely nothing like either my mom or Don. But now, I was willing to give good odds that if I ever met my biological father, the mystery of why I was the always the odd woman out in the Maxwell family portrait would be solved.

It was more than just physical differences between Sunny and me. Unlike my too-cute-by-half sibling, I was often vexed by our mother's free-range child-rearing philosophy. On some level, I had always wished my life had had more rules and structure instead of being guided by Mom's going-with-the-flow philosophy. As I became self-aware in my early adolescent years, I kept trying to find a boundary to cross that would provoke a reaction from Mom. From heavy metal music rattling the windows, to shaving part of my head and dying the rest of my hair purple, to shoplifting, to running with a bad crowd; nothing caused her to ever draw a line in the sand. To his credit, Don, on occasion, would have enough of my rebellious nonsense and lower the boom. But never Mom. Never even once. If anything, she was delighted that I was trying new things and new experiences.

My childhood had been a surreal nightmare.

Looking back, with ever widening parental guardrails, I could see why I grew up confused and miserable. Thankfully, I found refuge in my books. While nonfiction gave me a headache, fiction allowed me to enter other worlds, full of interesting people doing interesting things. I spent hours upon hours locked away in the safety of my bedroom while fully submerged in the gritty underbelly of society and traveling with no-nonsense, hard-boiled detectives as my guides. The more lurid the paperback, the more I liked it.

At thirteen I had an epiphany. I realized my goal in life was to get as far away from my mom and my golden-child sister as possible. With neither of my parents being particularly money motivated, I figured if I were to ever escape from Cincinnati, I would need to get an academic scholarship to a college far, far away. Starting my freshman year of high school, I put away childish things and focused all of my energy on my studies. Overnight, I went from troubled kid on a bad path to the valedictorian who blew the lid off of both her SAT and ACT exams, and was given a full ride to Columbia University in New York City.

Instead of being offended by my overt desire to be anywhere else but here, Mom, as usual, took my academic success as affirmation of her enlightened nurturing skills. *Give a child enough space and they will eventually find themselves,* was her belief.

What complete and utter bullshit was mine.

And nothing I saw in the five years since I put Cincinnati in my rearview mirror had shaken my resolve. Having spent so much of my time immersed in pulp fiction set in big cities, I always felt more at home in the Big Apple than I ever had in Midwest white-bread suburbia. I loved the noise and smells and the chaos of humanity swirling around me. It made me feel alive and connected.

The sound of Sunny's voice interrupted my little internal pity party.

"Your sperm donor was an interesting character," Sunny said as she continued to scroll on her phone. "Apparently he was some kind of mega enlightenment guru with everybody from movie stars to business tycoons flocking to his weekend seminars."

"Lovely," I said with a dismissive snort. "Where is he now? I'd like pay him a visit and kick him in his gurus."

"That's the interesting part," Sunny said as she furrowed her brow and read her screen. "Apparently, around the time Mom got pregnant with you, he disappeared."

"Disappeared? What do you mean, disappeared?"

"Just that. No one has seen him or heard from him for over twenty-four years," Sunny answered without taking her eyes off her phone. "Huh."

"Would you stop saying that?"

"Sorry." Sunny swiped at her screen again. "Did you know that this Peterson guy wrote three hugely popular self-help books and that Atonement Press holds the publishing rights to them?"

"Hold on," I said. "Are you saying that Simon Alphonse Peterson is S.A. Peterson? The S.A. Peterson?"

"That's what it says here," Sunny answered. "And if it's on the internet, you know it has to be true."

"Huh," I said, which brought a smile to Sunny's face. "I'll be damned. I always thought S.A. Peterson was a woman using her initials to hide her gender like J.K. Rowling, S.E. Hinton, or L.M. Montgomery."

"Apparently after he, she, or it vanished, an entire cottage industry sprang up with different theories about what had happened to him. They range from he's now a homeless guy living under a bridge in San Francisco to some of his followers claiming he ascended straight to heaven." Sunny turned her screen around so I could read it. It was a twenty-three-year-old headline from *Rolling Stone* magazine: "What Ever Happened to Mr. MAJIC?"

Underneath the headline was a black-and-white photograph of a man who, if I had to guess, would have been somewhere between thirty and thirty-five. Average height and not fat but also not particularly fit. He had a black Beatles-style haircut and dark sunglasses that were big enough and dark enough that it was impossible to see his eyes or even much of his face. Like me, he was compact with a dark complexion and had a pensive expression on his face.

Hello, Daddy.

CHAPTER THREE

AT THE FUNERAL home, Don, who had driven separately, had some final paperwork to deal with and told us he would be along shortly. Sunny and I migrated from the limo to my sister's old rattletrap of a car. The old rust bucket hadn't been much when she got it for her sixteenth birthday. Now, after five additional years of hard use and indifferent maintenance, the beater was about one pothole, hit dead center, away from needing its last rites. Because of the wake, the narrow street leading to our house was lined with cars on both sides, reducing it to a single lane. We had to stop twice to let other cars pass before we finally made it to the driveway.

When our neighborhood was being built, it was on the outer fringe of Cincinnati, where land was cheap and when gasoline was still less than thirty cents a gallon. If you were willing to drive a little, you got a lot more house for the buck than you could within the Cincinnati city limits. The developer who constructed our neighborhood, cutting costs wherever he could, had built all the houses close to the street. That way he didn't need to run water and sewer lines any farther than necessary. With each lot having at least an acre — ours had more than double that — it meant everyone had pretty impressive backyards. In the fifty-plus years since the first house on the street was built, the city had expanded and swallowed up our little slice of heaven. During my lifetime, we had gone from semirural to suburban to gentrified. All of the original owners had grown old and died, downsized after their kids had moved out, or migrated to a warmer climate. Mom and Don had been part of the first wave of replacements, and we had lived here since shortly after I was born. The neighborhood was in the process of turning over again, with the new arrivals being mostly young marrieds looking for good schools and a safe neighborhood to raise their kids.

Between kitchen appliance upgrades and bathroom remodeling, our local Home Depot was always hopping. I was told that heated in-ground saltwater swimming pools were the new status symbol on the street this year.

Our old clapboard two-story home was roughly the same size and shape as all the other 1970s cookie-cutter houses on the street; but ours was hard to miss. The rest of the homes were painted in earth tones with well-tended flowerbeds and neatly mowed lawns. Ours was a total reflection of my mom's free spirit. The exterior of the house was post-it-note yellow with whiter than white enamel trim around the windows, doors, and roof line. The front yard was a riot of rusty metallic "art," some pieces of which were taller than me, that Mom had repurposed in her workshop in the back of the house. Most of her raw materials had come from junkyard scraps and things she had found along the side of the road. She had welded them into occasionally interesting but, more often than not, ugly combinations. In addition to the large pieces, there were wind chimes and dream catchers hanging in the trees and on the corners of our wraparound porch. Along the south side of the house, what had briefly been a small Zen garden — until it became the favorite rest area for the local feral cats — was now an herb garden. Mom had put twigs and pinecones in the garden and planted lemon thyme to persuade the local felines to seek relief elsewhere.

The eclectic crowd of well-wishers had overflowed the house and had spilled out on to the porch and into the front yard. Other than a few stray friends of Sunny's from high school and college, who would offer their condolences then make a quick exit, there were three distinct groups, and it didn't take a program to sort them out. Don's friends were mostly blue-collar men and their families. The men were the strong silent types — the kind you could go fishing with, watch a game with, and count on to actually show up when you needed help moving. Guys with rough hands and soft hearts who were more likely to be drinking from a can of beer than sipping Chablis from a glass. Four or five of them were at one end of the porch, and their wives were huddled at the other end of the veranda trying to keep their high-strung offspring from maiming themselves on one of my mother's *objets d'art*.

Mom's friends — mostly female — were hippie throwbacks with lots of hair and long, flowing dresses. With their bright clothes and sandals, they were better dressed for a Woodstock revival than a solemn wake for a recently departed friend. The few men with them were middle-aged hippie wannabes who were too young to have been around in the 1960s and now were just embarrassing themselves. I would be hard pressed to decide who was worse: the guy north of fifty with a ponytail or the fortysomething with the lame attempt at a "man bun."

The last group — and by far the largest — was Don's family. Mom had been an only child and her parents, my grandparents, had been killed by a drunk driver when I was twelve. If Mom had any aunts or uncles or cousins, I didn't remember meeting any of them. Don, on the other hand, had a huge extended family, and most of them lived within walking distance from our house.

In my twenty-three-plus years of life on this planet, I did not have a single good memory of any interaction with members from that side of the family. Grandpa and Grandma Maxwell were standoffish to me until the day they died. My aunts and uncles always treated me like I had body odor and couldn't wait to get away from me. My cousins were all abusive and, despite me getting a full ride to an Ivy League college, while they struggled just to graduate from public high school, always acted as if they thought they were better than me.

With Don's friends boring, Mom's annoying, and my kin boorish, I was in no mood to be sociable. I got out of the car, avoided eye contact, and weaved my way through the throng to the stairs. Amazingly, I managed to make it safely to my old room and shut the door without having to engage with anyone.

I leaned my back against the now closed door and gently banged my head on it a couple of times. This was easily the worst day of my life.

With a sigh, I pushed away from the door and surveyed my old room. A flood of memories, some good, some bad, swept over me.

My mother worked in mysterious ways. Even though I had made it emphatically clear I never planned to permanently return home, she had kept my old room exactly the way I had left it the day I went off to college. With the blackout curtains Don had installed for me keeping out any hint of natural light, Sunny had always called my room the cave. For me it was an island of sanity where I could turn off the world and escape into my books. My eyes moved to the bookcase Don had built for me. Despite covering the entire wall from ceiling to floor and being over ten feet wide, the bookcase was still not large enough to hold my entire collection of trashy hard-boiled detective paperbacks. The strays were stacked on the floor and in boxes tucked in the odd corner. Dashiell Hammett's Sam Spade, Raymond Chandler's Philip Marlowe, and Rex Stout's Nero and Archie got me hooked. Being a ravenous reader, I soon added Mickey Spillane's Mike Hammer and John D. MacDonald's Travis McGee. Then Ross Macdonald's Lew Archer and Robert B. Parker's Spenser joined the long list of others.

It wasn't just pulp. Somewhere on my shelves, you could find nearly every book that had made *The New York Times*'s bestseller list in the past two decades. Mingled among the hard-boiled were favorite authors like Kurt Vonnegut, Tom Wolfe, Pat Conroy, David Morrell, Thomas Harris, Ian Fleming, Stephen King, Dan Brown, and a host of others.

During my teen years I briefly fell in love with Tom Clancy and had a passing fling with Robert Ludlum, and I still thought his *Road to Gandolfo* was possibly the funniest book I'd ever read. I worshiped Trevanian, but his book *Shibumi* was so damned good it spoiled me for that genre because nothing else ever measured up afterwards. I had a summer romance with J.R.R. Tolkien and was in my Hogwarts Gryffindor costume at the local Barnes & Noble at midnight for the release of the last Harry Potter book. I had a short-lived affair with lawyer books by James Grippando and John Grisham, but my heart always belonged to pulp fiction. Current favorites included old school Michael Connelly's Harry Bosch and Mickey Haller; Sue Grafton's Kinsey Milhone; and Lee Child's Jack Reacher — mostly because Reacher reminded me so much of Philip Marlowe. On rare occasions, when I was feeling my oats, I would imagine myself as David Baldacci's kick-ass assassin Jessica Reel. On less aggressive days, and depending on my mood, I would see myself as one of the members of James Patterson's Women's Murder Club.

When I needed a laugh, I'd grab a Janet Evanovich and sit on the edge of my seat waiting to see how zany bounty hunter Stephanie Plum would destroy one of Ranger's expensive cars this time. My favorite was when a garbage truck exploded and fell on her borrowed Porsche Boxster. Not far behind were when her friend Lula took out Stephanie's Monte Carlo with a rocket launcher and when Stephanie destroyed an outhouse, along with Ranger's Mercedes, after a boa constrictor got loose inside the car.

Since I was too embarrassed to lug any of them with me when I went off to college, I had left all my treasures here. After all, what would people think? It wasn't until I declared my major as English lit and started hanging out with kindred spirits that I discovered my affliction was fairly common in the Humanities Department. I was surrounded by people who loved a good story with characters you wanted to root for and villains you wanted to hate, and it didn't have to be written by Hemingway or F. Scott Fitzgerald. There were science fiction freaks, fantasy fanatics, chic lit aficionados, and even the stray zombie apocalypse fan. After we shared our wicked secret, I learned many of my classmates in my major had bookcases and boxes similar to mine back home.

I picked up a dog-eared paperback edition of a James M. Cain's *The Postman Always Rings Twice* and fell heavily onto my bed. As I sank into the soft cushion-top mattress I knew so well with a book in my hands, it felt like the warm embrace of an old lover.

Before I even got past the first Chapter, there was a light tap on my door, and Sunny poked her head in. "Your presence has been requested downstairs."

The hits just keep on coming.

CHAPTER FOUR

PPARENTLY I HAD lingered too long upstairs and had missed the famous Skyline chili dip made by our next-door neighbor, Mr. Henderson. It was a layer of cream cheese, covered with Cincinnati-style chili, sprinkled with minced onion, topped off with shredded sharp cheddar, and then zapped until bubbly. Throw in a bag of Fritos and you had, in my opinion, the perfect appetizer. Everyone else must have agreed. The Frito bag was down to the crumbs, and though I wouldn't swear to it, it looked like someone had run their finger inside the bowl containing the chili dip to get the last remnants. I had known Mr. Henderson my entire life. He was gruff but likable enough, I guess. I had often wondered whether he got his invitations to events like this based on his personality or the knowledge that he would always arrive with his Skyline dip in hand.

My nourishment options went downhill fast from there. None of the sympathy casseroles provided by Don's friends and his family looked appealing. They were mostly made from cans of condensed soup and piled over with greasy melted cheese on top to hide the mystery ingredients underneath. The "artisan" cheese and dried meat plates accompanied by organic gluten-free crackers presented by Mom's friends looked even less inviting. Having knocked around France for an entire summer a few years back, I knew what this stuff was supposed to look like. The Midwest Kroger deli version didn't even bear a passing resemblance to it. The sad-sack smorgasbord combined with the past six weeks of living in northwestern Wyoming — where the elk outnumber humans — had me just about ready to open negotiations to trade my first-born for a jumbo slice of Koronet Manhattan-style pizza. Lacking that, I had found my solace in an excellent bottle of Merlot.

Wine and an empty stomach had never been my best combination.

The filtration system that kept most of my more sarcastic thoughts safely inside my head instead of escaping through my mouth and pillaging the countryside only worked nominally well when my body was well-rested, well-nourished, and sober. At that moment, it was none of the above. Plus, I had had my fill of condolences from people whose faces I struggled to put to a name to. Because of the wine and the stress, I felt slightly off-center, and just being around all of these people brought back long-suppressed memories. Fearing a low-blood-sugar collapse, I grabbed one of the gluten-free crackers and took a tentative bite. It had the taste and texture of fossilized packing material. I wrapped the rest of it in a paper napkin and tossed it in the trash can as I surveyed the room.

I don't miss this place.

With no regrets, I had made a clean break and pretty much dropped all of the people, places and things from my old life down the memory hole. I had no interest in trying to locate a shovel to dig back up any part of it or them. Between college, summers backpacking through Europe and Asia, and now my new job, this was only my sixth trip "home" since high school. Counting the day and a half I had been here this time, it was only a total of sixteen days in the past five years.

I, of course, flew in for a weekend when Mom got the bad news six months ago. It was awful. Even Sunny seemed affected. When I was making the migration from Manhattan to Jackson Hole to start my new job, I had made a point to stop home and spend a few more awkward days with Mom. It was hard on me but even harder on her.

Everybody's first instinct was to do whatever was possible, from chemo to radiation treatments, but she refused. Her diagnosis of Stage 4 pancreatic cancer had focused her mind. She made me read an article by Dr. Ken Murray titled "How Doctors Die," and one sentence in the piece crystallized the circle of life for me: *They know exactly what is going to happen, they know the choices, and they generally have access to any sort of medical care they could want. But they go gently.* I wanted to stay longer, but Mom insisted I get on with my life. Even in her weakened state, it was tough to win any argument with her. That was so Mom.

I felt like I was ready to explode. Glancing at the clock on the wall,

I sighed. In another hour, two at the most, this would be over, and by this time tomorrow, I would be safely back to my new life as a line editor at a small press in Jackson Hole, Wyoming. It wasn't the highest-paying or most prestigious job in the world, but it allowed me to work around books and with writers. The only other job offers that my BA in twentieth-century American literature had brought before this had been working at Starbucks or waiting tables.

Fortunately for me, being an unapologetic Generation Z, I avoided the mistakes of the Millennials before me. I knew my major, my passion, didn't exactly have the highest market value. With that in mind, I buckled down and watched every penny. My scholarship was tuition and books only and did not include room and board. During my time at Columbia I worked part-time for minimum wage at one of the campus dining halls. While the job was well less than glamorous, my paycheck more than covered the cost of my housing and the big perk was I got free meals. When I graduated a semester early, I had a few dollars in the bank and an Ivy League diploma with zero student loan debt attached.

When Mark Franklin, senior editor at Atonement Press, had contacted me personally and requested that I apply, I was first over the moon, then baffled. Why would they want to hire a city girl like me to come out to the middle of nowhere where the nearest Target store or Trader Joe's was a hundred miles away on the other side of a mountain pass that had a nasty habit of being closed in the winter? How did they even know I existed? In the interview process, Franklin said I came highly recommended but was vague about who had made the recommendation. Still, I was so grateful to find work in my field, I didn't want to jinx it, so I never asked too many questions. I figured if I got some solid experience and added that line on my resume, in a couple of years I might be back in New York working for one of the Big Five publishing houses or at least maybe latching on with one of the major independent publishers.

Noticing my glass was nearly empty, I tottered in the direction of the kitchen in search of another bottle of Merlot and a possible raid on the refrigerator. I had noticed a LaRosa's pizza box on the fridge shelf earlier. While not in the same league as a New York-style slice, it would do in a pinch. Plus, I was hoping for a bit of privacy and maybe a quiet place to hole up until this nightmare was over. That dream vanished when I entered the kitchen and saw the last person I wanted to be alone with rinsing dishes at the sink: my know-it-all aunt Peggy.

How could this day possibly get any worse?

Then I found out how.

Tucked between the garbage can and the side of the refrigerator was an empty, oversized LaRosa's box.

"Damn you, Sunny," I muttered to myself. I downed the last sip of my wine in one gulp then slowly started to turn around to leave, hoping to make a quick, unnoticed exit.

Hearing movement behind her, Peggy glanced over her shoulder and smiled. "Well, there you are. If I didn't know better, I would have thought you were avoiding me."

Peggy Tucker — nee Maxwell – was the oldest of Don's five sisters and the poster girl for passive aggressive. She knew full well I had been avoiding her, since I had made a point of doing it my entire life. But, as usual, she couldn't resist taking a cheap shot.

After Grandmother Maxwell passed, Peggy – being the firstborn — had anointed herself as the family matriarch. She ruled her subjects with an iron hand. In her mind, there was no issue too large or small, with any member of the family, that couldn't be better served by seeking her wise council and blessing. She was only a notch or two short of being able to qualify as a character on *Game of Thrones*.

With short-cropped salt-and-pepper hair, she always had a pinched expression on her face like someone whose shoes were a half size too small and who had been on her feet all day. Since the last time I had seen her, her middle-age spread had gotten broad enough to apply for its own ZIP code. She wiped her hands with a towel, then gave me an awkward hug. "How are you holding up?"

"I'm fine."

"Donald tells me you're leaving tomorrow." Aunt Peggy was the only one on the planet who ever called my dad *Donald* — mostly because she knew it annoyed him, but she also knew he was too cowed by her to protest. Like I said: Poster girl for passive aggressive.

"I need to get back to my job."

"I see. I hope you'll come back again soon when you can stay longer."

I bit my lip and didn't say what I was thinking. In all likelihood, with my mom gone, the next time I would set foot in Cincinnati would either be for Sunny's wedding or Don's funeral. It certainly wouldn't be for a catch-up session with this old busybody.

Aunt Peggy's beady little eyes locked on me, and the corners of her mouth curled upward slightly. I had seen that expression on her face countless times and knew it was a harbinger of something nasty or cruel aimed in my direction. "All of this must have been a shock, especially the part about Donald not being your biological father."

"You knew about that?"

"Oh, honey," Aunt Peggy said triumphantly. "Everybody in town with a calendar and a lick of sense knew it."

I waited.

"As smart as you are," she added, "I'm surprised you never figured it out yourself."

There it is.

"How could I have figured out Don was not my father?"

"Seriously?" Aunt Peggy asked triumphantly. "You do know the dates of your birthday and when your mother and Donald got married, right?"

"Of course I do," I snapped.

My angry response brought a satisfied smile to Aunt Peggy's face as she moved in for the kill.

"You were born a bit over seven months after your parents eloped. Which was only a week after your mother got back to town."

"They told me I was a preemie."

Aunt Peggy shook her head and laughed. "Honey, there aren't a lot of babies born seven weeks early that weigh eight pounds, nine ounces. You were full term and then some."

I closed my eyes, mentally ran the numbers, then rubbed my forehead. The old biddy was right. I could have figured it out.

"Crap."

Aunt Peggy pointed a warning finger in my direction. "Language."

My mind-to-mouth filtration system was at least still partially functional; I swallowed "bite me, bitch" and held my hands up in mock surrender instead.

"That still didn't mean Don wasn't my biological father."

Aunt Peggy laughed. "No one had seen hide nor hair of your mother for almost a year before she showed back up." Aunt Peggy then did something odd; she awkwardly uncorked a wine bottle and poured herself a glass, then topped off mine like she was filling it with water instead of vino. Another half-ounce and my glass would have overflowed. It was entirely understandable that she would be a bit fuzzy on how much to pour. In all of my years being around her, I had never seen alcohol touch my aunt's holier-than-thou Southern Baptist lips.

"Did they tell you who your biological father is?" she asked coyly, with an eerie and unnervingly friendly tone in her voice that I had never heard before.

I studied Aunt Peggy carefully. While I was growing up, Sunny could do no wrong while I could do no right. Our aunt had never shown the slightest interest in me and, more often than not, had treated me like the hired help. Now it was clear why. Aunt Peggy had known all along I wasn't a "blood" relative, and being a little bastard had moved me to the back of the family bus. I wondered how long she had been wanting to drop this little bomb on me. I knew one thing for sure: Like all bullies, Aunt Peggy was a coward. She knew if she had let this secret out while Mom was still alive, there would have been hell to pay. Having no similar fear of her brother, it was now time for the dam of bile she had held back my entire life to burst.

The bitch is enjoying this.

Then it hit me. This sudden round of girl talk over a glass of Merlot was badly out of character. For the first time since I had gotten the call that Mom had passed, a smile formed on my face.

I took a defensive sip of wine to lower the fill level and savored the moment. "I was shocked when I found out how rich and famous he is. I can't imagine what it must be like to fly around in a private jet and rub elbows with movie stars and billionaires." I could feel the mischief flickering in my eyes and made no attempt to hide it. "Can you?"

Expecting to hear that my biological father was some lowlife loser, the kind of guy who would knock a woman up during a drunken Saturday night hookup and then vanish, Aunt Peggy was a bit startled by this news. But, to her credit, she recovered quickly. "No. Not really."

The old bat didn't have a clue as to the identity of my biological father but was dying to find out. Not knowing must have gnawed at her for decades.

Way to go, Mom!

Clearly Aunt Peggy hoped playing nice-nice might get me to lower my guard and reveal something. I licked my lips and savored the moment.

This passive-aggressive thing has real potential.

Aunt Peggy took a sip of wine, made a face, then put her glass down. She might have been evil, but she was also no fool. She'd heard me say how rich and famous he *is*, not *was*, so she assumed he was still alive and tried coming at me from a different angle. "Are you going to try to track him down?"

"How could I possibly do... Oh!" In my best Aunt Peggy impersonation, I feigned surprise and felt the corners of my mouth involuntarily moving upward. "You don't know who he is, do you?"

"I've always had my suspicions," Peggy answered with a hint of panic in her voice. She knew she had stepped in it and now was looking for an exit strategy, but there wasn't one.

I had her where I wanted her.

"Really?" I took another sip of wine and with glee called Aunt Peggy's bluff. "Who did you think it was?"

Aunt Peggy's eyes narrowed, and her smile vanished. Her face morphed back into the way I always remembered it while growing up: mean, vindictive, and judgmental. "You're exactly like your mother."

"I'm nothing like my mother."

"You only knew her after Little Miss High and Mighty had to slink back into town with a bun in the oven and conned my brother into marrying her," Aunt Peggy said with a snort. "She didn't turn into a flower child until after you were born and motherhood knocked off

some of her rough edges." She shook her head and sneered at me. "You remind me more and more of your mother every day."

"Why, thank you. That may have been the nicest thing you've ever said to me."

Aunt Peggy dumped her wine into the sink and stormed away. She arrived at the kitchen doorway at the same moment as Sunny and blew past her favorite niece without so much as a word.

"Nice to see you too, Aunt Peggy," Sunny said cheerfully to our aunt's back as it vanished into the thinning crowd of well-wishers before turning her attention in my direction. "You have an amazing capacity to piss her off."

"It's a gift," I answered as I took a healthy sip of wine.

Sunny poured herself some more Merlot, started to top off my glass, and laughed when she saw how full it was. "Drowning your sorrows?"

"Aunt Peggy poured it for me."

"Really? Why?" Sunny asked.

"She was trying to pry the name of my biological father out of me by being all lovey-dovey."

"Peggy? Lovey-dovey?" Sunny said with a laugh. "That has pay-per-view potential."

"It was a bit unsettling," I said with a laugh. "Speaking of lovey-dovey, what's the deal with you and Willie Hanson?"

"He prefers William these days."

"Are you two serious?"

Sunny wiggled her hand. "Too early to say, but I kind of like him."

"How long have you been dating?"

"He started pestering me to go out with him about five months ago, but I said no for the first couple of months because he really isn't my type."

"You have a type?"

"I usually find smart and creative people more fun to be around than geeks, but William can be a hoot."

"He certainly dresses nice enough. What does he do?"

"He has his own computer security company."

"Really," I said. "I remember him being really into music in high school."

"He was and still is. He plays the piano a couple of nights a week at the Pub just to unwind," Sunny said. "In fact, he just left and is headed over there right now."

"Is that where you ran into him?"

"No, actually. I came home one day, and he was helping Mom with a computer problem."

Great. My sister is semi-serious with an in-home tech support guy who dresses like a Wise Guy. Lovely.

"Speaking of Mom." I sighed and leaned against the sink. "I wonder what Don is going to tell us?"

Sunny made a face. "Ouch."

"What?"

"You find out he's not the sperm donor, and he goes straight from Dad to Don." Sunny shivered. "That's cold."

I extended my middle finger in the direction of my sister.

"Well, at least I'm still number one." A rare frown covered Sunny's face. "Seriously. This has been a lot to absorb in one day. You doing okay?"

I shrugged and took another sip of wine. "Peggy said I was just like our mom. I always thought you were her little mini-me."

"Daddy — sorry, Don…"

I made a face and flipped Sunny off again.

Sunny ignored me and continued, "…said Mom was a lot like you in high school but came back from her personal little *rumspringa* a different person. He has always called you BC and me AD."

"When did he ever say that?"

"Ah, like our whole lives," Sunny answered with a laugh. "With you being so busy tuning us all out for the past ten years, I'm not surprised you didn't hear it."

"What are you talking about?"

"Seriously?" Sunny took a sip of wine and shook her head. "After you reached puberty, you were a nightmare. First you were in that stupid punk rock band…"

"Heavy metal."

"There's a difference? Then you barricaded yourself in your room all through high school and you were on the first bus out of town the day after you graduated." Sunny shook her head again. "I don't think you said ten words to me the last four years you lived here. While you were in college, other than those uncomfortable phone calls we have on birthdays and Christmas, I bet you and I wouldn't have spoken to each other at all."

"That's not true. I may have not been the best half-sister in the world, but I wasn't that bad."

"Wow. Now I've been demoted from sister to half-sister." Sunny put her wine glass down with a clank. "Dad — I'm sorry, Don — has lost the love of his life and is about an inch away from unraveling right before our eyes. It's about time you pull your head out of your ass and get over yourself."

Sunny's eyes flashed with a glint of anger, and at that exact moment, the dishes Peggy had been rinsing clattered in the sink behind me, causing me to look in that direction. The stem on a wine glass had snapped under the weight of the other dishes and caused the stack of small plates to settle in the dish strainer. When I turned back, Sunny was gone.

CHAPTER FIVE

"Crap," I muttered as I put my wine glass down and moved in the direction of the kitchen door.

The crowd in the dining room and living room had thinned out, and the noise level had dropped noticeably. Apparently the abrupt exit of her royal highness, Queen Peggy, had sent the Maxwell clan scurrying out the door behind her. It also looked like all of Mom's old friends had abandoned ship as well. That left it down to a hard-core handful of Don's friends who, if history were a guide, would likely still be there until the last beer had been pulled out of the cooler on the front porch.

There was no sign of Sunny, but I had a pretty good idea where I would find her. As I turned toward the side door, I was cut off by Don.

"What did you say to Peggy?"

"As little as possible."

"Well, she left in a huff."

"When isn't she in a huff?" I answered with a snort.

"What did you say to her?" Don said slowly, but he was clearly losing his patience with me.

"She tried to pump me for the name of my biological father, and I pulled her chain a little."

"Today of all days."

"Look. She started in on me first."

"How?"

"She said I was stupid for not figuring out you weren't my biological father on my own. Then she insulted Mom…"

"What do you mean she insulted your mother?"

"She called her Little Miss High and Mighty who went out and got knocked up, then conned you into marrying her."

"Peggy said that?"

"Yup. Then she said I reminded her of Mom."

"Then what did you say?"

"I told her that was the nicest compliment she had ever given me."

Don held out his fist for a knuckle bump. "Nice. Why did Sunny storm out?"

"I don't think she liked it when I called her my half-sister."

Don Maxwell shook his head, closed his eyes, and rubbed his forehead. "You're certainly like your mother in at least one way. She never held back on letting you know exactly what she was thinking either." Don looked around the room. "I'm going to run everyone out of here. Go try to make peace with your sister and I'll be along in a few minutes. I have something to show both of you."

"Okay," I said. As he started to walk away, I pulled him back. "I'm sorry about being such a baby earlier."

"Forget about it," he said as he gave me a hug. "This has been a tough day all around." He kissed me on the top of the head. "Go work things out with Sunny."

I slipped out the side door. The air was crisp from a Canadian high pressure system that had swept all of the clouds, July humidity, and normal air pollution across the Ohio River to south of the Mason-Dixon line. Two days short of being full, the moon cast a ghostly silvery glow on the well-worn path weaving into the woods behind our house. Not that I needed the illumination. I had walked this route so many times that, even after five years, I could probably do it blindfolded. As I rounded the last bend, up ahead was the old barn bordering the outer edge of our property line. I smiled when I saw the flickering light through the window and open door. Mom's old workshop had gotten a fresh coat of paint since the last time I had seen it. Since this had been her favorite spot in the entire world, I figured Dad — wanting to do something, anything, to make her final days as happy as possible — had spruced it up for her.

That was so typical of him.

I smiled when I noticed he had left the sign Mom had hand-painted years ago, above the door. Now faded by the sun, it had been there for as long as I could remember.

Happiness Equals
Forgive, Forget and Release

In the middle of the old building, Sunny, wearing a welder's mask and heavy gloves, was working on what appeared to be an old bicycle frame. I stopped and gasped. From thirty feet away, it would have been easy to mistake Sunny for our mother. Sunny was half a foot taller but moved the same way Mom always had.

Seeing me coming, Sunny powered down her welding arc and flipped off her mask and gloves. "I'm sorry I lost my temper." She held me at arm's length and examined me from head to toe. "You okay?"

"Of course," I answered with a puzzled expression on my face. "Why wouldn't I be okay?"

"When I was in high school, whenever I lost control of my emotions, the person I was mad at got a leg injury."

"What are you talking about?"

"Remember Christie Long?"

I shrugged. "Barely."

"Well, she pissed me off, and as she was walking away, she stumbled and broke her ankle."

"And that was your fault?"

"Remember Billy Ross?"

"That stupid jock who embarrassed you in front of the whole school at halftime of the homecoming football game your sophomore year?"

"Yeah. He blew his knee on the first play of the second half."

"Coincidence."

"Then, after you left town, that little creep Frank White spread some nasty rumors about me because I wouldn't go out with him. After I confronted him, on his way home, he totaled his dad's car and suffered a compound fracture of his leg."

I shook my head in disbelief. "You really believe you caused all of those injuries?"

"Once is happenstance. Twice is coincidence. Three times is enemy action."

I chuckled. "Quoting Auric Goldfinger to justify your insanity doesn't help your case."

"I never even noticed the pattern until Mom pointed it out. Since each injury was to the legs and each was worse than the previous one, she was afraid if I kept getting angry, the negative energy my psyche was throwing around might kill somebody."

"Wow. I would expect that level of nonsense from Mom, but I can't believe you're buying it too."

"We are only as blind as we want to be."

I laughed hard for the first time in days, and it felt good. "First using Ian Fleming and then Maya Angelou against me, that's cold."

"Just because I'm not a twentieth-century American lit major like some people doesn't mean I haven't read a few things," Sunny said with her normal disarming smile. "Buy it, don't buy it; that's up to you. But ask yourself this question, what are the odds that the only three people to make me lose my temper in four years of high school all ended up with leg injuries?"

I put my hands on my head to keep my skull from exploding. "And you wonder why I couldn't wait to get away from this loony bin. Look, I'm sorry about the half-sister thing and calling Dad, Don."

"Forget it," Sunny said cheerfully. "I get it. Your little cheap shot at me was small potatoes. I've already fully released it. Once things calm down around here and you've headed back to your job and I can get myself fully or properly centered again, I'll release you as well."

"Whoa, whoa, whoa. Are you talking about one of Mom's kick-somebody-to-the-curb releases?"

"Exactly," Sunny answered matter-of-factly. "I'd always held out hope that we would be closer, but now I can see that will never happen. After the incident in the kitchen, I realized I had given you power over me, and now that I'm aware of it, I won't let it happen again," Sunny said with a smile.

"What happened in the kitchen?"

"I let you cause me to have an emotional reaction for the first time in a long time, and things started breaking. I knew I needed to get out of there before I hurt you."

"What have you been smoking, little sister?" I shook my head. "You honestly believe your special spidey sense broke the wine glass?"

"How else do you explain it?"

"Oh, gee, let me think. The glass stem was already weakened, and Aunt Peggy stacked heavy plates on it."

"Okay," Sunny said with a radiant smile. "That just proves my point about us being so far apart that we're never going to be close," she said without even a whisper of animus toward me. "I knew with Mom being gone, one of the few threads that still connected us had been severed. With the way you've reacted to discovering Dad is not your biological father, it is clear we no longer have anything in common." Sunny hugged me and kissed me gently on the cheek. "Have a wonderful life and I hope you find happiness and inner peace."

CHAPTER SIX

I WAS STUNNED. MORE than stunned; I was stupefied.

"What are you saying? You never want to see me again?"

"Good heavens, no. We're still sisters, and there is no reason why we can't continue to have a cordial relationship. You know, calls on birthdays and Christmas. Same as always."

"So does this mean because I was an ass to you and Dad, you hate me now?"

"The opposite of love is not hate, Grace. The opposite is indifference. You can get as nasty as you want to be toward me, but that doesn't mean I have to care."

"What the hell are you talking about?" I objected.

"Because of social pressure, often the toughest things in life to deal with are the complications of family relationships. You're constantly being thrown into contact with people who provoke a negative response. Earlier tonight, hopefully unconsciously, you sent a shot across my bow with the sole intent of hurting my feelings and trying to provoke a reaction from me." Sunny shook her head. "Sorry. I won't give you that kind of power over me."

"What is this power you keep talking about?" I demanded.

"Look at Aunt Peggy. Instead of being indifferent toward her, you let her get into your head, which gave her the power to make you miserable."

"So, you're saying Aunt Peggy being mean to me is my fault?"

"Finally, you're starting to get it!" Sunny said with a laugh. "By nature, Peggy is a manipulative bitch whose life's ambition is to make everyone around her as miserable as she is. Mom told you to ignore her. I told you to ignore her. But you would never let her go and have paid a heavy emotional and spiritual price. So yes, on some level, your problems with Aunt Peggy are all self-inflicted. You've always had the power to kick her fat ass to the curb anytime you wanted to, but you seem to prefer to wallow in self-pity rather than be happy."

"Easy for you to say since Peggy has always adored you."

"Everybody adores me," Sunny answered with a laugh as she batted her eyes in my direction. "FYI. If you would drop your negative defensive shields and take a more positive approach to life, people would like you more too."

"People like me," I protested.

"Sure, the ones you let inside the fortress." Sunny laughed again. "Because of the negative energy you spit out pretty much twenty-four-seven, the general consensus is you're a stuck-up bitch and a head case."

"Nice."

"On the flip side, it was my fault I let you get to me tonight. I wanted so badly for us to be close I tried to force it, and that never works."

"So, you're saying we're at an impasse?"

"Maybe," Sunny said with a laugh. "Look, it is pretty simple. I want to live my life like Mom while you want to be exactly like Aunt Peggy."

"Don't you dare lump me in with that shrew!"

"It only stings because you know what I'm telling you rings true." Sunny shrugged. "You let Aunt Peggy get into your head, and your inability to ignore her and your instinct to fight back are what has shaped you into what you are today."

"Which is?"

"Miserable, adrift, and overthinking everything." Sunny leaned on Mom's workbench. "Life is pretty easy if you don't go all manic depressive and get too high on the good days and too low on the bad ones. Take charge of your life and if you don't like the path you're on, try a different one."

"Meaning?"

"Aunt Peggy knew she could jerk you around and you would respond in kind, which just encouraged her to abuse you more, and you've been in that escalating vicious cycle ever since."

"Good grief. You're sounding more and more like Mom."

"Thanks! If someone, including a family member, is not making your life better, you need to release them so they have no power over you. But on some level, you already know that."

"I do?"

Sunny snorted and giggled. "Of course you do. You used the crudest and most primal release imaginable. You moved away. Out of sight, out of mind."

"You're saying me going away to college was like one of Mom's 'releasing exercises' she kept trying to make me do?"

"Sort of. Except you never released anything; you just buried it. It is still there, and being here brought it all rushing back in living color." Sunny smiled and shrugged. "You can run away, but you can't hide from yourself. No matter how hard you try to avoid it, eventually the stuff you don't release will come back and get you."

"How do I figure out what to release?"

"Release everything. Then when something truly worth hanging on to comes back, with your mind clear of all the noise and clutter, you'll recognize it. Aside from that, just let the bullshit flow through you and it's all good."

"Now you're putting me in the BS category?"

Sunny sighed. "At this moment, I'd have to say yes."

"Lovely."

"Look. You've got a good soul and a good moral compass, but you're carrying so much self-imposed emotional baggage, it is exhausting to watch. I get that you and Mom were on completely different wavelengths. But to Mom's credit, she knew there are many paths to inner peace, and we all need to find our own way." Sunny's eyes filled with tears. "You were always too pigheaded to realize the incredible gift Mom gave you."

"Gift? What gift?"

"For someone so smart, you can be so stupid."

"Now you're starting to sound like Aunt Peggy."

"Yikes!" Sunny said with a laugh.

"What gift?"

"Mom knew being around her — and, by extension, me — was making you miserable. She loved you so much she was willing to let her firstborn child walk out of her life forever if that was what it would take to make you happy."

Sunny's words hit me like a thunderbolt. It was one of those moments of perfect clarity when suddenly everything made sense.

"Wow," I said gently. "I never thought of it like that."

"Obviously."

"Any suggestions on my personal self-improvement?"

"Meditation would be a good start."

I rolled my eyes so hard that, combined with a bit too much Merlot, I nearly lost my balance. "I have a confession to make, but I don't want you to get too full of yourself," I said with a sigh.

"Oooh!" Sunny leaned in closer. "Do tell."

"I've actually tried a few of Mom's techniques."

Sunny punched me in the shoulder. "You little rascal. Did you tell Mom about it before she passed on?"

I snorted. "I didn't have to. She brought it up the moment I walked in the door. She said she could see a difference in me."

Sunny laughed. "That was so Mom!"

"Tell me about it. I was making some progress, but Mom dying and this whole Peterson thing has really knocked me off stride, and I feel like I'm back at square one."

"Sudden emotional shocks can throw anyone off the path to enlightenment." Sunny said cheerfully. "Would you like some suggestions to get back on track?"

"I would love it," I answered. "I've tried a few yoga classes, and they were a complete joke."

"You need to stay away from those places that are only interested in what yoga pants you're wearing. Plus, none of it is necessary."

"No?"

"No. You are not going to find your way just by taking the right yoga class or giving your money to the right guru. A spiritual quest is one hundred percent personal. Remember that old Woody Guthrie song Mom used to sing to us?"

I hadn't thought about that in years. "You've got to walk that lonesome valley."

"Exactly. Nobody else can walk it for you."

I looked up at Sunny. For the first time in my life, I felt like I was seeing her for who she truly was, and I mentally kicked myself for having wasted two decades resenting her.

Sunny, of course, immediately saw the change in me and bounded over and gave me a hug and chuckled. "Ohh, look at you!"

"How did you know what just happened?" I demanded.

Sunny replied, in a terrible Chinese accent, "Ah, Grasshopper. One must learn to walk before one can fly."

I burst out laughing. "What the hell does that mean?"

Sunny started giggling. "I have no idea. I just made it up."

Sunny pulled me closer, and we laughed together for the first time since we were little girls. It felt wonderful.

"Look," Sunny said as she finally pulled away. "Try this. It's quick and easy and super useful. It is called the Coherent Technique." Sunny made me square my shoulders. "Breathe a little slower and more deeply than usual and focus on a good thought or something that makes you happy. While doing that, imagine air is flowing in and out of your chest in the area around your heart."

"How long do I do it?" I asked.

"I do a four count in and out," Sunny answered, "but do whatever works for you."

I did as I was told and had to admit I felt better.

"Again."

I felt the tension leaving my body and even the ever-present tightness in my shoulders and neck began to relax a little

"That's amazing," I said as I flexed my neck.

"Do that every time you feel your body tensing up," Sunny said cheerfully. "The beauty of that technique is that it doesn't require being in a lotus position or repeating some boring mantra. You can do it anytime and anyplace. You can do it while reading, driving your car, sitting at your computer."

"How often should I do it?"

"I do it about ten times a day when things are going well and a lot more often when things suck."

"Really? I never noticed."

"Why should you?" Sunny said with a laugh. "I've been doing it for so long that it comes naturally for me and I don't even notice it myself."

"What else have you got?" I asked.

"Every night when I go to bed and every morning when I wake up, I use a method called the Heart Lock-in."

"Really? Heart Lock-in?"

"Don't knock it until you've tried it."

"Okay, okay," I said. "How does it work?"

"It can take from five to fifteen minutes, and you need to find a nice quiet spot with no distractions or interruptions. That's why I do it in bed."

"Okay."

"Shift your focus away from your mind and imagine that you're breathing slowly through your heart."

"Breathing through my heart?"

"Trust me," Sunny said. "After a few cleansing breaths — ten, maybe fifteen seconds — start remembering someone you love or someone who is having a positive influence on your life. Try to stay with that feeling for as long as you can. When your thoughts start to intrude and your mind begins to drift, or you feel blocked, gently bring your focus back to your heart. All the while be softly sending thoughts of appreciation to those you love and to yourself."

"That's it?"

"Yup," Sunny answered. "I've always used Mom as my focus." Sunny's face brightened as she looked past me. "Here comes the perfect person for you to use."

Turning, I saw Dad headed in our direction with something in his hands. "What's he carrying?" I asked.

Sunny's eyes grew large, and she gasped. "It's Mom's magic box!"

CHAPTER SEVEN

DAD WAS APPROACHING the workshop with an ornate and very old looking lacquer box in his hands.

Sunny pointed a warning finger in my direction. "If Mom left that to you, I swear you'll need crutches for the rest of your life."

I closed my eyes and shook my head. "I'm pretty sure she would have left her most prized possession to her little clone and not her absentee love child."

Dad stopped in the doorway and sighed when he saw the expression on Sunny's face and the way she was eying me. "Don't worry, your mom didn't want the two of you pulling each other's hair out on the day of her funeral over her silly little box. She had a compromise."

"Compromise?" Sunny and I said in unison.

Dad sighed again. "Yes." He held the box out between the two of us. "Sunny, you get the box."

"Yes!" Sunny shouted as she broke into a happy dance and reached for the box, but our father pulled it back.

"But," Dad said as he handed the box to me, "your sister gets the contents."

"What?" Sunny protested. "All I get is an empty box while Morticia Addams here gets to finally see what's inside?" Sunny folded her arms across her chest. "That sucks."

I leaned in and whispered to Sunny, "Draw in air through your heart…"

Sunny slugged me in the shoulder.

"As usual," Dad said with a tired sigh, "when it came to anything involving your mother, I didn't get to make the rules, I only get to follow the ones she decreed."

I gave the box a little shake, and clearly there was something inside.

"Well?" Sunny demanded. "Are you going to open it or not?"

"For heaven's sake, Sunny. It's just a damn box," I snapped. "Don't pee your pants."

"My entire life, Mom never kept anything secret from me, except what was inside her magic box," Sunny said. "I was always tempted to take a peek when she wasn't looking."

"That's why after you turned ten and developed a sneaky streak, she kept it hidden from you," Dad said.

"Where did she hide it?" Sunny demanded. "I looked everywhere for it."

"She moved it around a lot, but it has been in the same spot for the past five years."

Sunny motioned for Dad to continue. "Where was it?"

"Remember the dress you wore when you won homecoming queen?"

"That hideous thing?" Sunny gasped, and her eyes flew open wide when she realized the magic box had been in the bottom of a dry cleaner bag in her own closet. "That's cold."

Dad and I started laughing. "No, Little Sister," I said, "that is one hundred percent a Mom move."

"I've always wanted to know what was in it." Sunny began bouncing up and down. "Open it! Open it!" she said in a whiny voice.

I shook my head before turning to Dad. "Do you know what's in here?"

"Not a clue."

"Come on," Sunny pleaded. "Open it!"

"Jeez." I said and extended the box toward my sister. "Clearly it means a hell of a lot more to you than to me. You open it."

Needing no additional encouragement, Sunny snatched the box out of my hands and fiddled with the elaborate brass latch until the lid opened with a loud creak. There was a small note that was too far away for Dad or me to read sitting on top of a neatly wrapped package. Sunny's lips moved slightly as she read the note, then she started laughing so hard tears formed in her eyes. "I am going to miss Mom."

"What does the note say?" I demanded.

Sunny tried to read the note but couldn't control her giggles, so she handed it to our father. Dad's eyes danced across the note, and he joined Sunny in laughing.

"What does it say?" I repeated.

Dad cleared his throat and regained his composure. "It says, 'Sunny, give the box back to your sister.'"

"She knew me too well." Sunny said as she returned the box to me.

In the bottom of the box was an envelope with *Grace* written on the outside. Checking to be sure there was nothing else inside, I handed the now empty box back to Sunny. "All yours."

Sunny absently accepted the box and placed it on Mom's workbench but never took her eyes off the package in my hand.

"What's that?" she asked breathlessly.

I just shrugged and turned it over and examined it. It was a large, oversized manila document envelope sealed with ancient and yellowing cellophane tape that had what felt like the better part of a ream of typing paper inside. Nothing else besides my name was written anywhere on the outside of the envelope. I opened the envelope, and as I removed the stack of papers from inside, a golden drinking straw fluttered out and onto the ground.

We all laughed. Mom knew both of her daughters too well. My favorite bedtime story when I was a child was one she had made up and called "The Little Girl and the Golden Straw." Basically, every time the little girl, Serenity, would have a bad day, her mother would give her a magic golden straw when she went to bed. Serenity would pretend she was sticking the straw into the middle of her chest, then squeeze all of her problems into a tight ball and let them shoot out the straw, and they would never bother her again. I liked it because Mom kept changing the storyline to fit all of my prepubescent problems, which kept the story fresh and personal.

My entire life, at every meal and with every beverage, Mom always gave me a straw.

Sunny picked up the golden straw, blew any potential dirt off of it, and handed it back to me. She nodded at the stack of papers. "What's that?" Sunny asked.

I tucked the straw in my pocket and leafed through the papers. "It looks like a manuscript of some kind."

Dad moved to my left shoulder, and Sunny moved to my right, and the three of us examined the title page.

The True Path of Enlightenment
by
S. A. Peterson
&

Elizabeth Morris

"Cheese and crackers," Dad muttered under his breath before turning to me. "I'm beat, and I've had about enough of this guy for one day. Can we talk about all of this in the morning?"

"Of course," I said as I gave him a hug. As he started to release his grip, I pulled him back in tighter and whispered in his ear, "You'll always be my daddy."

Tears welled up in his eyes as he pulled away and held me at arm's length, then kissed me gently on the forehead. Without a word, he turned and left Sunny and me alone in the workshop.

"Nice," Sunny said as she gave me another playful punch in the shoulder. "Keep that up and I may have to rethink this whole releasing-you thing and actually put in some effort into staying in touch."

"Releasing can be a two-way street."

"Meaning?"

"Now that I'm figuring out how to do the whole releasing thing myself, Dad will always be Dad. The jury is still out on whether I want to keep you around or not."

"Hey!"

I examined the manuscript. "Interesting," I said, "that Mom would have her name listed as co-author with Mr. MAJIC."

"Oh no!" Sunny shouted as she looked at the manuscript and started laughing so hard she had to support herself on the workbench to keep from falling over. "Mom had a wicked since of humor."

"What do you mean?"

"This wasn't her 'magic' box with a *G*. It was her 'majic' with a *J*. It had Mr. MAJIC's manuscript inside."

I started laughing too. Sunny was right.

That was so Mom.

"What do you make of this?" Sunny asked as she wiped a tear from her eye.

I shrugged. "The publishing house I work for holds the rights to all of Simon Alphonse Peterson's earlier books."

"So you've said," Sunny answered, not seeing where I was headed.

"He wrote a trio of huge-selling self-help books years ago, but I don't remember this being one of them."

Sunny rechecked the title to be sure she had it right, then her fingers danced across the screen of her iPhone. "This manuscript was never published… Oh my… but there were all kinds of rumors that it existed before Peterson went AWOL."

"Really?" I said as I looked at Sunny's screen.

"If this guy was such a big deal," Sunny asked as her eyes unfocused, which, I knew from experience, meant her brain had just clicked into overdrive, "how did a boutique small press in the middle of nowhere like yours get the rights to his books?"

"Excellent question and I know just the person to ask."

Fishing my own phone out of my pocket, I hit the speed dial.

"Who are you calling?" Sunny asked.

"My editor…" I held up one finger as the line was answered, then pressed the speaker button so we both could hear.

"What do you want, Maxwell?" said the gruff voice of Mark Franklin, senior editor of Atonement Press. Franklin was old school and didn't have a politically correct bone in his body. His bluntness and lack of tact had made his co-workers at the Big Six — now Big Five — publishing house where he used to work uncomfortable, but he was too damn good at his job for his boss to ever reprimand him, much less fire him. Rumor had it, after Peterson's disappearance, the bloom was off of his rose in New York and the long knives were out looking to take his scalp. He finally had had enough of the office politics and took a job with the newly formed Atonement Press. The rumor also was, Franklin got to pick where to locate the office and he selected a spot about as far away from the NYC culture as you could get: Jackson Hole, Wyoming. Now in his late fifties and after twenty-four years at the helm of Atonement Press, Franklin had slowed down a bit and considered himself semiretired. He now only worked half days — twelve hours.

"What do you know about S.A. Peterson?"

"Other than editing his three books?"

It looks like that part of the rumor was true.

"Really?"

"Why are you bothering me, Maxwell?"

"Have you ever heard of a book of his called *The True Path of Enlightenment?*"

"Yeah. I've also heard of Santa Claus and Big Foot, and they don't exist either. Why?"

"I have the original manuscript in my hands."

"Of course you do," Franklin said with sarcasm dripping from every word.

"I'm serious."

"How the hell would a pissant less than a year out of college and with six whole weeks of publishing experience get her hands on the Holy Grail of self-help books?"

"Holy Grail?"

"People have been looking for that manuscript since before you were born, Maxwell. If it ever goes to press, it would blow the top off every bestseller list in the world."

"What?"

"To this day, Peterson is our bestselling author, even though no one has seen or heard from him in over two decades. Last year we sold over two hundred thousand print copies of his books and five times that in eBooks." Franklin snorted. "Imagine what his long-lost manuscript would do. We'd have to do a five, maybe even ten million hardback run, and the paperback edition would empty Oregon of trees. And it would be anybody's guess how many mountains would have to be topped to get enough coal to power all the eBooks it would sell."

"Seriously?"

"It would be the publishing event of the year. Hell, maybe the decade. What makes you think you have the manuscript?"

"It turns out Peterson is my biological father."

"You know this how?"

"My mother left me a note that he was my father."

Franklin snorted. "From time to time we get delusional offspring of ex-hippies and damaged yoga chicks showing up claiming to be Peterson's love child and asking for money. I'll tell you the same thing I tell them."

"What's that?"

"Prove it."

"How can I prove it?"

"Exactly, Snowflake." Franklin said with another snort. "His kid or not, until you have iron-clad proof you have Peterson's missing manuscript, no one — and I mean no one, including us — will touch it."

"What kind of proof would you need?"

"Short of Peterson himself suddenly resurfacing and claiming credit, I can't think of anything else that would make it worth the risk."

"If this book could be that big, don't you even want to see it before you dismiss it out of hand?"

There was a long silence. "Do you have access to a scanner?"

I looked over at Sunny, who nodded.

"Yes."

"I have some of Peterson's original manuscripts in a box somewhere. Send me a pdf of the first ten pages and I'll compare them. If it looks promising, I'll pass it along to the boss. Good night, Maxwell."

The line went dead.

"What an ass," Sunny said.

"Yeah," I answered, "but for some unknown reason, he has taken a personal interest in me, and I've learned more about the real world in the last six weeks working with him than I did in twelve years of public school and three and a half years of college."

CHAPTER EIGHT

"**M**an," Sunny said as she lifted the lid and exchanged the page on the glass plate of our mother's scanner for another one. "This thing could be on *Antiques Roadshow.*"

I had always remembered our mother's "office" as being a disaster area with books and papers stacked everywhere. Now, the only things on her desk were her computer and her old four-in-one printer/copier/fax/scanner. The bookshelves were neat with the titles alphabetized. The trashcan was empty, and the desk drawers were organized and free of clutter. The space had the look and feel of the handiwork of someone who had spent their last few months getting their affairs in order and didn't want to leave a mess behind for bereaved loved ones to deal with.

"That's interesting," I said as I thumbed through the manuscript.

"What?"

"It has Mom's handwritten notes all over it."

Sunny removed a page from the scanner and, before replacing it on the glass, did a double take. "Huh." Sunny handed the page to me. "It looks like Mom's boy toy was going to dedicate his book to her." She pointed at a line of text that read, *To Elizabeth Morris, who shined the light on the true path of enlightenment.*

And written with a fine-point Sharpie, in bold block letters underneath the dedication, were the words, *I owe you more than you'll ever know.*

I flipped the page over, held it up to the light, and closely examined the backside of the manuscript page.

"What are you looking for?" Sunny asked.

"I want to see whether some of the ink has bled through the paper."

"This is important, why?"

I just shrugged. "Mr. Franklin always does it to see whether he has an original or photocopy."

"Again. Why?" Sunny asked absently as she changed the page on the scanner.

"He figures with us being a small press, a long way from nowhere and near the bottom of the publishing food chain, if somebody sends him a photocopy, they've probably already sent it to fifty other places that have rejected it, and he doesn't give it much of his time."

"I guess that makes sense," Sunny said, then added, "I've got the first ten pages scanned."

Sunny pushed our mom's keyboard in my direction, and I attached the pdf to an email in my Google account. "Here goes nothing," I said as I hit the send key.

"Now what?" Sunny asked.

"We wait for Mr. Franklin to get back to me."

"More wine?"

"You need to ask?"

We were nearly to the door when my phone rang. The caller ID indicated it was from Atonement Press. "That didn't take long." I hit the answer button and then the speaker button. "Hello…"

Franklin, talking louder and faster than necessary, cut across me. "How many people have read this manuscript?"

"Read? As far as I know, it has been in a box on my mom's shelf since before I was born, and we only found it half an hour ago. I would say no one has read it for over two decades."

"How many people know this manuscript exists?"

"So far, only you, my father, sister, and me." I felt a tingle go up my spine. "Do you think it's real?"

"I was the line editor for Peterson's three other books, so I know all of his writing habits and quirks. If it is not his work, then it is the greatest forgery of all time."

"Whoa," Sunny muttered.

Franklin continued, "Is Lizzie Morris your mother?"

Lizzie?

"Yes," I answered. My head was spinning. "Did you know her?"

"We met a few times back in the day and Peterson raved about her," Franklin said excitedly, then moved back on point. "If this proves to be genuine, it will certainly buttress your case for claiming Peterson is your father, but, after reading what you've sent me, it also amped up the verification of authenticity needed."

"Why?" I asked.

"If the rest of the book is anything like the first ten pages, then this is a complete refutation of Peterson's first three books."

"I don't understand."

"I take it you haven't read the heading to the introduction yet, Maxwell."

"No."

"I also take it that you haven't read any of Peterson's earlier books."

"My mom gave me one of them years ago, but non-fiction makes my eyes glaze over so I never got past the first couple of pages."

"Smart girl. Peterson was the consummate salesman and showman who found his shtick in the self-help industry. His seminars, with lights and projection screens, were years ahead of their time and something to behold. When I was editing his books, and I would want to make a change, he would always refuse. He told me he had a team of psychologists and marketing people who had carefully selected every word for maximum impact. With that in mind, read the intro heading."

I pulled the page out of the stack and gasped when I read it.

> *Is your guru doing you more harm than good?*
> *Why are you taking spiritual advice from a guy you wouldn't buy a used car from?*

"Oh my."

"Exactly. From what I've seen so far, it looks like Peterson was writing his confessional. Without iron-clad confirmation of authenticity, if we publish this, it will look like a cheap-shot hit piece on a cultural icon and would get us laughed out of town."

"What do you want me to do?" I asked.

"Scan the rest of the manuscript and email it to me as soon as possible."

"We're using an ancient scanner without a page feeder so it will take us a while."

"Us?"

"My younger sister is helping me."

"Can we trust her to not blab anything about this to her friends?" Franklin asked.

Sunny burst out laughing. "Grace can trust me a whole hell of a lot more than some shriveled-up old prune she's only known for a couple of weeks."

"You didn't mention she was on the call, Maxwell," Franklin said gruffly. "Is anyone else in the room?"

"No," I answered.

"Just us girls," Sunny added sweetly.

"I can't stress enough how important it is, if word of..."

"We're not idiots," Sunny said, cutting across him with a rare edge in her voice that surprised me.

I shot Sunny a funny look, then continued, "We get that this is potentially a big deal. Sunny already knows about the manuscript, and I trust her to be discreet."

"All right. All right," Franklin said. "Then we..."

Sunny cut across him again. "I have a few questions for you."

"Such as?"

"I understand Atonement Press owns the rights to Peterson's previous books; is that correct?"

"Yes," Franklin answered.

"How did you acquire those rights?"

"Let me guess," Franklin said gruffly. "Prelaw?"

"She scored one hundred seventy-six out of one hundred eighty on her LSAT exam and starts Yale Law in three weeks," I said.

Sunny made a face and whispered in my ear, "How did you know that?"

"Mom told me." I leaned in closer. "She was really proud of you."

"Ahh. So sweet."

The voice of Mark Franklin on my phone broke the spell of our little bonding moment. "I don't like being interrogated," he said tersely.

Sunny laughed. "If you want to see the rest of the manuscript, you'll find a way to get past that, won't you? How did you acquire the rights?"

"Can I assume that is not going to be your last question?" Franklin asked gruffly.

"Nope," Sunny answered confidently. "I'm just getting warmed up."

There was about a five-second delay before Franklin spoke again. "I'll need to get authorization from Nathaniel Goodman before I can reveal any terms of the agreement with S.A. Peterson."

"Who is Nathaniel Goodman?" Sunny asked.

"He's the owner of Atonement Press, among many other things," I answered.

Sunny's fingers moved quickly across her iPhone's touchpad, and a startled expression covered her face. "Holy crap; he's one of the most generous philanthropists in the world. How come I've never heard of him?"

"Mr. Goodman has always been a bit camera shy and likes to keep a low profile," Franklin answered. Then he continued, "I'll call you back in a few minutes." The line went dead.

"Who are you, and what have you done with my kid sister?" I asked, a bit befuddled by Sunny's personality shift from Pollyanna to Perry Mason. "You sound like a veteran prosecutor, not some kid just starting law school."

Sunny just laughed. "The last semester of my senior year, I was only six credits short of my degree so, to keep from going stir crazy, I got permission to take some graduate level law courses."

"Graduate level law courses?"

"Specifically, Contract Law and Ethical Business Negotiations."

"Why in the world did you pick those classes?" I asked

"Once you learn how to turn off the static in your mind, you will have a sense of what to do to make your life better."

"A sense?" I asked with a pronounced eye roll. "Seriously?"

"My sense told me I needed to take those classes." Sunny shrugged. "And here I am using what I learned."

Before I could arrange for a visit to an exorcist to deal with my kid sister's felt "sense," my phone rang again. It was Mark Franklin.

"Much to my amazement, Mr. Goodman has authorized me to answer any and all of your questions."

Sunny morphed back into a hard-nosed interrogator. "How did Atonement Press acquire the right to S.A. Peterson's books?"

"Mr. Goodman purchased the reprint rights shortly before Peterson disappeared. He planned to use the proceeds of the sale of the books to fund the publishing of important works about philosophy, religion, enlightenment, and self-help that wouldn't have a big enough audience to get another publisher otherwise. Around the time Peterson disappeared, Mr. Goodman established Atonement Press and recruited me to run it."

"Do you or your publishing house own the rights or have first right of refusal for this manuscript?"

"No, but…"

"I assume, after over twenty years missing, that Mr. Peterson has been declared legally dead," Sunny continued.

"I have no idea," Franklin answered. "But since he had no spouse and no known heirs, I'm not sure anyone would have bothered."

"In that case," Sunny said in a businesslike tone, "if he is your bestselling author, where are the royalty checks for his books going?"

"Excuse me?" Franklin asked.

"Contract law 101 — follow the money," Sunny whispered to me, then turned her attention back to Franklin. "It was a pretty straightforward question, Mr. Franklin."

There was another long silence, then Franklin cleared his throat. "The royalties have been deposited into the escrow account for Mr. MAJIC Inc.," Franklin answered.

"And who controls Mr. MAJIC Inc.?"

"Nathaniel Goodman," Franklin answered.

"Interesting," Sunny said. "Why haven't the funds been distributed to corporate shareholders?"

"There is only one shareholder, Nathaniel Goodman. He has wanted to keep the funds intact in case Peterson or an heir ever surfaces."

"Why would he do that?"

"You would have to ask him," Franklin answered.

"I'll rephrase," Sunny answered. "Why do you think Mr. Goodman left all of the money in the escrow account?"

Franklin sighed. "I'd prefer not to speculate."

"I would prefer if you did," Sunny responded. "I'm sure you have an opinion, and I want to hear it." Sunny paused. "Let me remind you, Mr. Goodman has already, in your words, authorized you to answer any and all of my questions."

Franklin sighed again. "I've always suspected Goodman let the account grow in the hope that the balance would eventually be large enough to encourage Peterson to reappear."

"You said earlier that Goodman was holding the funds intact if Peterson or an heir ever surfaces. If my sister can prove paternity and establish herself as Peterson's only heir, will all of the funds in that account belong to her?"

"She would have to satisfy Mr. Goodman of the validity of her claim…"

"And," Sunny cut across Franklin yet again, "since Mr. Peterson has no known heirs and my mother bequeathed this work to my sister, wouldn't that mean Ms. Grace Bliss Maxwell would hold the sole rights to this manuscript?"

"I would have to run it past our legal department," Franklin answered. "But, since this book was outside the scope of our original agreement with S.A. Peterson, I would assume she would hold the unencumbered rights."

I had never seen this side of my sister before. Her combativeness and aggressiveness were one hundred eighty degrees opposite of her normal demeanor and were more than a bit unnerving.

"Since you have no claim to the rights to this manuscript while my sister clearly does, doesn't that mean she is under no obligation to have this manuscript published by your company and we could shop it to other publishing houses?"

There was another long silent pause. "Yes," Franklin answered softly. "Is that your intention?"

"Naw!" Sunny said with a laugh. "I'm just messing with you."

Suddenly, the Sunny I knew was back.

"Grace would be an idiot to take it to a different publishing house. You know Peterson and his work better than anyone, so it would likely be impossible to prove the manuscript is legitimate without your help. With that said, you still might want to modify your attitude toward my big sister. If we can prove paternity, she will have a strong claim to not only this manuscript, but the rights to all of Peterson's royalties held in escrow." Sunny paused for a moment to let this new reality sink in. "Grace Maxwell is no longer the least senior member of your staff but is potentially your most important client."

There was another long pause. Then I heard something I never expected to hear in my lifetime. Mark Franklin, no-nonsense curmudgeon, started laughing. At least I think it was laughter since it was somewhere between the sound of a machine gun and a dog hacking up a sock it shouldn't have eaten.

It was even more unnerving than watching Sunny verbally slapping Mr. Franklin around.

"I like you, kiddo," Franklin said when he regained his composure. "We're going to get along great."

"We'll get along better," Sunny said, "if you never call me kiddo again."

"Your sister has already claimed Maxwell; what do you prefer?"

"Sunny will do nicely. Thanks."

"Let's get back to the manuscript," Franklin said briskly. "Scan it as soon as possible and email it to me. Then find a safe place to keep the original until I can have it picked up and brought to me."

"Is that necessary?" I asked. "I'm flying back tomorrow."

"No, you're not," Franklin corrected.

"I'm not?" I protested.

"You tell her, Sunny."

Sunny put her hand on my arm. "You're going to be staying here in Cincinnati and spending the next few days trying to get proof Peterson is your father and the manuscript is real."

"I knew I liked you, Sunny," Franklin said. "Get me the copy ASAP." The line went dead.

CHAPTER NINE

USING THE SLOW single-page flatbed scanner, it took the better part of two hours to convert the nearly three hundred pages of the manuscript and accompanying notes into a pdf and attach it to an email. It probably could have been done in less time, but after we pulled the cork on the second bottle of Merlot, Sunny and I devolved from the perpetually overachieving Maxwell girls to the giggle sisters.

It started off slow with idle chitchat, then, as we both began to realize we really liked each other, all bets were off. We compared notes on the first time we each got drunk, laid, and stoned. We agreed Mom must have been something in the sack for Dad to have taken her back pregnant, then to put up with all of her nonsense for all those years. We also agreed if there were more men like Don Maxwell, the world would be a much better place.

Sunny confessed that she loved following in my wake through high school. "My freshman and sophomore years were amazing. You had everybody so intimidated, no one had the nerve to ever mess with me because they thought it might be like releasing the Kraken."

We spent twenty minutes talking about all of the pranks we had pulled on our extended family, particularly Aunt Peggy and her three dreadful boys.

"Then," Sunny said, "after Aunt Peggy's evil spawn bragged about egging our house, I put super glue in all of the keyholes in Cousin Eddie's car."

"I got blamed for that!" I protested.

Sunny batted her eyes at me. "Of course you did!" Sunny put her hands under her chin, tilted her head and manifested the most insincere smile imaginable. "Me bright and perky. You dark and foreboding."

I slugged her in the shoulder. "You awful and evil!"

"What are you complaining about? It added to your legend."

"You could have told me you did it," I protested.

"That would have required us to actually have a conversation instead of spending four years glaring at each other," Sunny answered.

"I must have been a real delight to live with back then."

"A real beacon of joy," Sunny said.

Then it started. First as a chuckle that rattled my chest. Then, as my laughter began to build, it became contagious and infected Sunny. I felt tears starting to form in my eyes. "Eddie was so pissed."

Sunny, laughing and wiping a tear from her eye, said, "I know. It was great!"

Despite the late hour, we were getting too rowdy. Dad, his hair a mess, walked into Mom's office to be sure we were both okay. Looking first at Sunny, then at me, he just shook his head and, without a word, reclosed the door.

Sunny, panting as she tried to regain her composure, glanced over at me. "You and Dad going to be okay?"

Before answering, I used Sunny's breathing technique, focused on my heart instead of my head, slowly drew in air, and then released it. Sunny nodded her approval.

"Dad and I will be fine. We'll talk, and he'll understand."

"Of course he will," Sunny said. "Besides, this 'who's your daddy' conundrum is interesting, but you need to remember this whole shared DNA thing is highly overrated."

"Meaning?"

"It is much better to hang out with people who actually love you and make you happy than ones who are related to you that make you miserable."

"Speaking of DNA, do you think this Peterson guy is really my biological father?"

"I've never known Mom to lie…"

That made me laugh loud enough that I checked to be sure Dad wasn't coming back in to ground me. Mom had been a merry prankster with a knack for saying just the right thing at just the right time to let the air out of an overinflated ego. A punster and the master of the double entendre, she had the ability to get Aunt Peggy whirling like a dervish. While her lies were often whimsical and too outrageous to be taken seriously, to her, "truth" was subjective and a matter of perspective.

"Let me finish," Sunny objected. "I've never known Mom to lie when it came to the important stuff." Sunny shook her head. "But thinking this guy is your father and proving it are two very different things, especially when it comes to the kind of money we're talking here."

"What kind of number do you think we're looking at?"

"You're asking me?" Sunny said with a laugh. "You're the one working for the publisher."

"I only work on the content side. The publisher and accounting people make all of the financial decisions."

"Really? Why?"

"There is a lot of ego in the book business. To keep our authors from getting their noses bent out of shape when they find out someone got a bigger advance than them, we are like Fight Club. The first rule of the terms of a book contract is you never discuss the terms of a book contract."

Sunny scratched her head. "Franklin said they are still selling over a million copies of Peterson's books every year. At only a buck a book for the author, that's a cool million a year times twenty years in the escrow account. Plus interest."

I whistled. "That would be a lowball number," I said. "I'm sure he was selling a lot more copies twenty years ago than he is today. It could easily be ten times that or even more."

Sunny whistled then nodded in the direction of the stack of paper next to the scanner. "And that doesn't include any advance and royalties you would get for this manuscript."

"That's not me, it's we. If anything comes of this, it will be a three-way split."

"Ahh, that is so sweet," Sunny said with a smile. "But let's not spend any of it yet. Trying to prove paternity from someone who has been missing for over two decades is going to be damn near impossible. It's not like we can go ask for a lock of hair, cheek swab, or blood sample."

Before I could respond, my cell phone rang. The caller ID said *Atonement Press*. I answered it, then put it on speaker.

"Yo."

"This is clearly Peterson's work," Franklin said.

"You're certain?"

"I'd bet my kid's inheritance on it," Franklin answered.

"Hold on," Sunny said as she made a face. "According to Wikipedia, you've never been married and don't have any children."

"That made it a pretty low-risk bet on my part, don't you think?"

"You didn't tell me he was funny," Sunny said.

"Who knew?"

"I've looped your buddy Mr. Goodman into this, Maxwell," Franklin said.

"Buddy?" I protested. "I've only been in the same room with him once, and there were so many other people throwing elbows trying to meet him, I didn't even get to shake his hand."

"That's surprising," Franklin said. "Especially since he's the one who insisted I interview you. You're going to be getting a visit from a private investigator named John Cutter who will help you with your search."

Sunny did another web search, then leaned in and whispered. "Unless he's moonlighting as a proctologist from Poughkeepsie or a plumber from Tulsa, he doesn't exist online."

"What makes John Cutter so special?" I asked.

"He's an expert on all things Peterson. Goodman hired him when Mr. MAJIC went missing, and he has been on a retainer ever since," Franklin said.

"What's the deal with 'Mr. MAJIC?'" Sunny asked.

"It was Peterson's stage name and a complete rip-off of The Beatles's *Magical Mystery Tour*," Franklin answered. "Legend has it, Peterson got the idea for his entire empire when he heard Don Henley's *Boys of Summer* lyric, 'I saw a Deadhead sticker on a Cadillac.' Peterson saw a niche audience of nostalgic middle-aged ex-hippies with disposable income, pining for the good old days and trying to find meaning in their lives."

"There are rumors all over the internet that Mr. MAJIC had a secret meaning, like The Beatles's 'Lucy in the Sky with Diamonds' spelling

LSD," Sunny said.

"Nothing nearly that clever, I'm afraid. Peterson was a suave businessman. Initially he changed it from 'Magic' to 'Majic' to avoid any potential copyright infringement suits. After that was decided on, Peterson used it to brand himself. His first book was '**M**oving to **A**cceptance, **J**oy, **I**nsight and **C**larity,' which has sold over one hundred million copies and got him the Mr. MAJIC moniker. He played on that theme with his next book — and a direct rip-off of a Lovin' Spoonful song — *Do You Believe in MAJIC?* Fortunately, John Sebastian was a big fan of Peterson and licensed the rights to the song for peanuts. It was the opening number of every session of his road show. The last book, *Real MAJIC*, was just a cut-and-paste rehash of the first two books. After the initial pop in sales, it didn't have the staying power of the first two books. MAJIC Inc. had run out of things to say and lost some of its luster. Combine that with the rest of the self-help industry starting to mimic his showmanship and Peterson's core audience was moving on to the next new hot guru flavor of the month. Then there was the bad press."

"Bad press?" I asked.

"Apparently the staff and crew of his seminars became legendary for their wild drug-fueled parties, often with young women. It was a running joke with his production crew that MAJIC actually stood for 'Mushrooms, Acid, Joints, Idiots and their Cash.'"

"So, it was all a con job?" I asked.

"I don't know if I would go that far. There are millions and millions of people who claim Peterson's techniques changed their lives," Franklin said. "Plus, there is the old publishing apologue that no author is a genius to his editor. I was his editor, and I got to see all of the warts, not just the polished finished product." Franklin sighed. "His books were fine, and this new manuscript is nothing short of brilliant. It was his road show that I found vulgar."

"Why?" I asked.

"I guess by today's standards, they were pretty tame; but back then, they were something to behold. They used music cranked up loud enough to affect the inner ear and give the audience a sense of euphoria. Big-screen visuals, pyrotechnics, wireless microphones so they could walk around on the stage. They had plants in the audience to get everyone to cheer at the right times. Plus, Peterson was riding the perfect storm."

"What perfect storm?" Sunny asked.

"The economy was good, and the baby boomers who were approaching their midlife crises had money in their pockets. Thanks to a constant stream of stories about Catholic priests molesting little boys and the church covering for them, evangelicals ripping off their congregations, and a president screwing any woman who got in his field of vision, faith in many major social institutions was at an all-time low. People were looking for something to hang on to, and Peterson threw them a lifeline."

"Right time, right place, right message, and right person," I said softly as I tried to absorb all of this new information.

"Exactly, Maxwell," Franklin said.

"It sounds like you knew him pretty well," Sunny said.

"I barely knew him at all. Despite his huge public persona, he was a near total recluse. We're talking Howard Hughes level here. I edited all three of his books, and I never met him face to face. If I remember correctly, I only spoke to him on the phone once or twice."

I shook my head in disbelief. "How is that possible?"

"When he wasn't at one of his weekend events, he was always in New York. We exchanged hard copies of the manuscripts via bike couriers, and we communicated almost exclusively through CompuServe."

Before I could ask what the hell Franklin was talking about, thus making an idiot of myself, Sunny leaned in and whispered, "CompuServe was Google and Facebook's great-grandfather."

"Look," Franklin said. "First thing in the morning, I'm going to teleconference with Mr. Goodman and legal and see where we stand on this end. But I already know what they're going to say. While I believe this is Peterson's work, we don't have nearly enough to publish this manuscript with his name on the cover. John Cutter should be a big help. He has retired to Hendersonville, North Carolina, which I understand is only four or five hours' drive from you. I called him right after you sent me the first few pages. Hopefully he'll be there sometime tomorrow. Until then, you should start looking for any concrete proof of paternity or find a provenance for that manuscript. Without that, we're dead in the water."

CHAPTER TEN

"Where do you think we should start?" I asked as I surveyed the room and sighed.

"You're the big mystery reader, not me," Sunny answered.

Sunny had a point. From my reading, I should be good at this. But in mystery novels, everything always seemed so simple and logical, and there was a narrator to help move things along. Out here in the real world, I was clueless.

"We could talk to Dad," I offered.

We both dismissed that immediately.

"I think he has reached his Mr. MAJIC limit for the day. Maybe even forever," Sunny said.

"Agreed," I answered.

Then, at the same moment, our eyes locked on Mom's MacBook Pro. Sunny, who hated technology as much as I did but was better at it, jumped into Mom's old chair, pulled the Mac in her direction, and squared it with the edge of the desk. She typed in a password, and immediately it opened to Mom's homepage.

The wallpaper was a picture of Sunny and me when we were little girls.

Sunny rubbed her hands together as she read the icons on the screen and nothing looked very helpful. She tapped the Finder icon in the taskbar at the bottom the screen, then opened All My Files.

"Huh," Sunny said as she scrolled through the files.

"Really?" I said. "I thought we had moved past that."

"Sorry," Sunny answered. "It's just there is almost nothing on the hard drive."

"How is that possible? She had that Mac for years."

"No idea," Sunny answered. Then she snapped her fingers.

"Unless…" Sunny dove back into the files.

"Unless what?" I demanded.

"Unless she moved all of her archives to the cloud."

"Why would she do that?"

"No idea… Unless." Sunny changed the Finder to organize by date instead of name. "Damn it. There is nothing older than six months on here."

"Okay," I asked warily. "That means what?"

"Six months ago is when Mom brought William in to work on her computer."

"You think your boyfriend set Mom up with a cloud account?"

"One way to find out."

"Which is?"

"We could ask him." Sunny glanced up at the clock in the top corner of the laptop screen and saw it was approaching midnight. "Let's go."

"Go where?" I asked.

"I told you earlier, he's sitting in with a friend's band at the Pub tonight. The last set will be over around one o'clock."

I glanced at the wine bottle and shook my head. "I'm in no shape to drive, and neither are you."

"It's only a little over a mile from here, and it's a beautiful night. Let's walk."

"Okay, but I'm going to visit the little girls' room first."

"I'll meet you by the front door in five minutes," Sunny said as she headed out of the office.

I made my way up the stairs and into the bathroom next to my bedroom. Looking in the mirror, I saw I was a hot mess. I glanced in the direction of my make-up travel bag, then back at the mirror, and instantly realized there wasn't nearly enough firepower in that tiny bag to make much of a difference. I brushed my teeth, ran my brush through my hair, and muttered a silent prayer that I wouldn't see anyone I knew as I headed back downstairs.

When I saw Sunny at the bottom of the steps, I was reminded that she was one of the most beautiful females I'd ever seen. She never wore look-at-me outfits or accessories. She never fussed endlessly with her hair.

She looked better rolling out of bed first thing in the morning than I could ever hope to look after an hour of preening. All the social-climbing girls in high school hated her since she set the bar so high for the rest of them. Sunny never seemed to notice and, more importantly, never cared enough to allow herself to get swept up in their petty nonsense. Instead the "mean girls" were left trying to keep up with a rival who didn't even bother to participate in their small-minded games.

"You ready?" Sunny asked as I joined her in the foyer.

Self-consciously running my fingers through my hair, I answered, "As ready as I'll ever be."

We stepped outside to a beautiful star-filled night and started the short trek to the local watering hole officially named McClinton's Wild Irish Brew Pub. The newcomers called it McClinton's while to the old-timers like us, it was just the Pub.

"What's it like in Jackson Hole?" Sunny asked.

"First off," I answered with a laugh, "it's Jackson — adding the Hole immediately brands you as a tourist. Second, I'm still in the adjustment stage."

"Adjustment?"

"I moved from New York City with a population of over eight million to a town with a permanent population of less than ten thousand."

"That has to be a cultural shock."

"Not as bad as you might think. They pretty much took the best of NYC and compressed it down. There are great restaurants that would compare well against anything Manhattan has to offer, some amazing art galleries, and a marvelous performing arts center."

"Really?" Sunny made a face. "I had no idea."

"With two world-class ski resorts and two national parks in Teton County, there are a lot of really rich people with amazing homes there. But the biggest difference is the level of fitness of the people who live there." I smiled at Sunny. "With your little skinny butt, you'd fit right in."

"Too cold and snowy for my taste."

"I wouldn't know since I haven't had to deal with a Jackson winter yet, but the summer has been nothing short of amazing — no humidity, almost never gets above eighty during the day, and drops into the fifties at night. I've never seen skies that blue. At night it is so clear you can actually see the Milky Way and satellites moving across the sky."

"Really?" Sunny said. "How much snow do they get?"

I sighed. "Last year, nearly six hundred inches."

"Good Lord," Sunny said with a dismissive shake of her head and a shiver.

We arrived at the Pub, and the parking lot was less than half full, but one of the cars caught my eye. Parked in a back corner, taking up two parking spots, was an Aston Martin Vanquish with vanity plates that read *HACKER 3*.

"That's some car."

Sunny glanced at it and dismissed it as she reached for the door. "That's one of William's."

"One of his cars?"

Sunny rolled her eyes. "He has a six-car garage at his house and rents space for the rest of his fleet somewhere near his office. Normally I would say it was a cry for help for his sexual inadequacy, but I know better."

"And how exactly do you know that?" I asked.

"Shut up," Sunny answered with a silly grin.

"What does Willie do again?"

"William," Sunny corrected. "Computer security."

"Are you sure he doesn't deal drugs or something else questionable to afford a car like this?"

"He recently sold off one of his companies for like a bajillion dollars, but he still has an office in Silicon Valley and some place in Europe and a couple hundred employees."

"So, exactly what is a guy with a bajillion dollars, offices on two continents, and a car that cost more than I make in four years doing working on our mom's home computer?"

"Excellent question," Sunny said as she pulled the door open. "Let's ask him."

The Pub was pretty much how I remembered the place, and the crowd was pretty much what I would expect this close to last call on a weeknight. With the kitchen shutting down hours earlier, most of the tables were empty except for the three closest to the stage where Willie Hanson was in the middle of an impressive riff on the piano. Sunny waved to a large man I didn't recognize who nodded in her direction. He was sitting by himself with his back to the wall and, oddly, with his eyes pointed at the door and the bar instead of the band.

Only two of the eighteen barstools were empty; the rest were occupied by the hard-core drinkers. Without any place better to go, they looked like they had been on their stools for hours. At the sound of the door opening, all heads turned in our direction. A time-worn, but still attractive, woman sitting at the far end glared at us as she calculated that her odds of any more offers of free drinks tonight had just grown slimmer. The sight of Sunny, and maybe to a lesser degree me, caused all of the men at the bar to snap to attention.

Our bleary-eyed cousin, Eddie Tucker, Aunt Peggy's eldest son, was sitting between two of his old high school buddies, Dave Davis and Fred Dibble. He leaned forward to size up the new arrivals. Fleshy with pink skin that didn't see much sun, Eddie looked like he had added an average of one pound a month since he graduated from high school five years ago. Dave and Fred weren't too far behind in the weight department, and, despite only being in their mid-twenties, all three looked like they were only about three minutes on a Stairmaster away from needing a coronary bypass.

A twisted evil smile covered Eddie's face as he pushed himself to his feet and headed in our direction.

Crap.

Sunny grinned when she saw Eddie approaching and leaned in to me. "Watch and learn."

"Meaning?" I asked.

"You saw the way I handled your Mr. Franklin."

I knew it. Her personality shift when she was talking to Mr. Franklin was an act.

"This will be a good opportunity for you see how I deal with annoying family members and keep them from having any power over me."

"What are you going to do?" I asked.

Sunny glanced over at the man sitting alone at the table across the room, smiled, and nodded. The man saw Eddie heading in our direction, and instantly his eyes narrowed, and he was on his feet. "When you don't give anyone power over you, life is a hoot. You might want to take notes, big sis."

"Well, well," Eddie said with a slight slur to his voice and more loudly than necessary, causing all of the bar birds to take notice and shift on their stools for a better look. "If I had known it was little bastard night, I'd have worn a tie."

I immediately felt my blood pressure rising and was about to take the bait until I saw the twinkle in Sunny's eyes as she stepped between the approaching Eddie and me.

"Any night you're here isn't 'little bastard night,' Eddie. It's obviously 'big fat-assed bastard night,'" Sunny said sweetly. "I mean, what else would you call a guy who parks his butt on a bar stool for five hours when he's got a wife at home who's eight and half months pregnant, other than a bastard?"

I wasn't sure where Sunny was headed, but I liked the direction she was going and got into the swing of things.

"I'd call him a total jack hole," I offered.

"Dick wad?" Sunny suggested.

"Douche bagel?" I recommended, which drew a look from Sunny. "What? I read it somewhere."

"You're not very good at this, are you?" Sunny said, which drew chuckles from Eddie's posse.

"For your information, I just talked to Jill, and she is just fine..." Eddie stopped when he saw Sunny staring at the front of his shirt. "What?"

"Did you enjoy your chicken wings?" Sunny asked.

Eddie examined the front of his shirt but didn't see anything.

"Made you look!" Sunny said brightly. "Besides, seeing how big you've gotten since high school, clearly you don't let much of anything miss your mouth."

Dave and Fred were struggling not to laugh but were losing the battle. The rest of the barstool brigade didn't bother to show the same restraint.

Eddie's face darkened when he heard the snickers of his peer group behind him. Clearly, his anger was starting to reach the danger zone.

Eddie had a history as an ugly drunk, and I was starting to get worried. "What are you doing, Sunny?" I muttered. "You know how Eddie gets after a few drinks." For reasons unknown to me, Sunny didn't share my concern.

"You're punching way above your weight class with that one, Hoss," Dave Davis offered.

"I can handle her." Eddie said with more confidence than he actually felt. He had tangled with Sunny before and still had the scars to prove it. Knowing his huff and bluff had never worked on his attractive cousin, he started looking for an easier target. Eddie turned his attention in my direction. "I'm surprised you'd have the nerve to even show your face in public…"

"We're here to celebrate!" Sunny said brightly, turning Eddie's focus back to her.

"Celebrate what?"

Sunny put her hand on her chest, and a baffled expression covered her face. "Are you kidding? I am so jealous of Grace right now I could just scream!"

"Why are you jealous?" Eddie asked suspiciously.

"Duh!" Sunny shouted loudly enough even the band stopped playing and she had the undivided attention of everyone in the room. "Because your uncle Don is not her biological father!"

"So?" Eddie answered.

"Don't you get it? Unlike me, Grace doesn't share any of your DNA! That's better than winning the Lotto!"

Everyone in the room, except Eddie's wingmen, who were suddenly fascinated by their half-empty drink glasses, erupted in laughter. Eddie's face turned bright crimson, and he started opening and closing his fists as if he was seriously contemplating punching Sunny in the mouth.

There is an old saying: When your only tool is a hammer, all problems start looking like a nail. Eddie had been a bully, a nasty drunk, and not much else worth mentioning for as long as I'd known him. With Eddie, brute force was the only thing in his toolkit; and with him, you could win the verbal battle but still end up stuffed in a locker. While it took more to provoke him to hit a girl than a boy, it had happened more than once. Sunny was tiptoeing close to a line better not crossed.

But Sunny wasn't done yet.

"I see you're still running with your old high school chums." Sunny made a face like she was trying to remember something. "What did you guys call yourselves?"

Dave Davis turned toward Sunny. "We were Davis, Dibble, and Turner. D-D-T. Dy-na-mite."

"Huh," Sunny said with a disappointed expression on her face. "I thought it was Eddie, Dave, and Frank. E-D-F. Erectile Dys-Function."

That did it.

Eddie took two quick steps toward Sunny and drew back his open hand to slap her when an amazing thing happened. The blow never landed. Instead a powerful hand clamped down on Eddie's right wrist and spun him around so fast and so unexpectedly it caused our tipsy cousin to lose his balance and end up flat on his back on the bar floor with a stunned expression on his face. Standing over him was a stone-cold-sober, six-foot-three-inch man in his late twenties with a short-cropped military-style haircut but without an ounce of fat on his two-hundred-twenty-pound frame.

"Didn't your mommy ever tell you it's not nice to hit girls?" the man hissed softly, then pointed a warning finger at Dave Davis, who was starting to slide off of his stool to come to the aid of his friend. "You might want to rethink that," the stranger said softly as he opened his coat to reveal a Glock 21 clipped to his belt as he rested his hand on the automatic's grip.

CHAPTER ELEVEN

THE BAR WENT quiet, and Dave Davis froze as his eyes locked on the automatic. Over the years, he and his running mates had been in more than their share of bar fights, and three against one was always their preferred ratio. But even with eighty-six-proof courage flowing through his veins, he was sober enough to know you never want to arrive empty-handed to a gun fight.

Eddie used a chair to brace himself as he scrambled to his feet and glared at the stranger. "Who the hell are you?" he demanded.

Sunny gave the stranger's arm a squeeze, then kissed him on the cheek. "This is my guardian angel. Well, he's William's guardian angel actually, but Harrison is good at multitasking."

Willie has a bodyguard?

"You don't scare me," Eddie said.

"Then you're an even bigger idiot than I thought," Sunny said brightly, which brought another ripple of laughter from the bar birds.

Sunny had a point. Harrison definitely looked ex-military and not the kind that parked their butt in headquarters where their biggest risk of injury was a paper cut. He reminded me of a dozen antiheroes I had met in my novels. A tough, no-nonsense guy with a soft spot for a dame in distress. Exactly the kind of guy you didn't want pissed off at you just before last call in a bar.

Eddie, getting his first real look at Harrison, saw the same thing, and hesitated. "Anybody can sucker punch somebody," Eddie said defensively.

He should know; he's done it often enough.

Eddie, foolishly decided to prove his point. He glanced away, then threw a wild roundhouse in the direction of where he expected Harrison's chin to be. Unfortunately for Eddie, Harrison hadn't fallen for that old trick since second grade. He easily sidestepped the blow and then delivered an open-handed slap to the left side of Eddie's face with enough force that it staggered my brutish cousin, who nearly went down for the second time. Welts in the shape of a hand formed on Eddie's cheek, and I suspected they were distinct enough for a good forensic person to pull a full set of Harrison's prints.

"First off," Harrison said softly, "if I had sucker punched you, you'd be on your way to the ER and getting prepped for facial reconstructive surgery. All I did was stop you from slapping a girl and then watched you fall on your fat ass all by yourself. Second of all, because I'm working, I just let you off easy after you tried to sucker punch me. As fat and slow as you are, I could have given you a shot to the kidney that would have you pissing red for the next week." Harrison winked at me and grinned. "Instead I gave you exactly what an overstuffed douche bagel like you deserved: a bitch slap."

Eddie, with his hand pressed to his burning cheek, stared at Harrison for several seconds and calculated his odds. They didn't come up in his favor. His pride had been wounded, but he was out of options.

The tension was broken by the voice of Sunny's boyfriend. "I think we've had enough fun for one evening." William Hanson tossed a pair of hundred-dollar bills on the bar. "Let me pick up your tab and we all can call it a night."

"What if we don't want to leave?" Eddie sneered.

Dave Davis looked at the grinning Harrison and, from what he had seen so far, had the distinct impression that, with or without a gun, the bodyguard could mop the floor with all three of them and not even muss his hair. He grabbed Eddie by the arm and started to tug him toward the door. "Come on, man, it's getting late. Let's go home."

Eddie tried to pull away from Davis, but Dibble joined in, and the pair maneuvered Eddie toward the door. The further he got from Harrison, the braver and louder Eddie got.

"This isn't over. I'll see you again."

Harrison blew Eddie a kiss. "Bring your own body bag."

Hanson leaned over to Harrison. "Go and be sure they don't key my car."

Harrison nodded, and as he took a step toward the door, the Dynamite boys picked up their pace and scurried outside with their tails firmly between their legs.

I slugged Sunny in the shoulder. "You wouldn't have been such a smart mouth if you weren't confident you had backup."

Sunny laughed then shrugged. "You still don't get it. The universe provides us with everything we need. Tonight I had Harrison on my seven."

"What?" I asked.

"He had my back."

I shook my head. "You mean he had your six."

"Whatever," Sunny said with a dismissive wave of her hand.

Hanson chuckled. "Hey, Grace."

"Hey, Willie."

Hanson chuckled again. "No one has called me that in years."

"Sorry. Sunny told me you prefer William these days, but old habits die hard."

"In your case, with our track record, Willie will be just fine."

"Huh?" Sunny said as her eyes bounced back and forth between Willie and me. "Exactly how well did you two know each other in high school?"

I fanned myself. "It got hot and steamy the summer between our junior and senior years," I said matter-of-factly.

Hanson, to his undying credit, immediately caught on. "And a good chunk of our senior year as well," he added.

"Eww," Sunny said as she made a face and confronted her boyfriend. "You never told me you dated my sister."

Hanson and I both burst out laughing.

"Grace couldn't stand the sight of me in high school," Hanson said. "Which was unfortunate since we were in so many of the same classes."

"You were amazingly annoying," I said.

"Your hostility was weird since I don't recall ever doing anything to you," he said.

"Ha!" I shouted. "You never took a single note. I never even saw you open a book."

"So?"

"Meanwhile I'm busting my butt while you sat in the back of the room nodding off like you were bored out of your skull."

"I was bored," Hanson answered. "Fortunately, I hooked up with some kindred spirits at Stanford, and the rest is history."

"What's the deal with the bodyguard?" I asked.

Hanson shrugged. "When we spun off our retail security division…" As he saw the blank look on my face, he elaborated, "We created tools to help prevent credit and debit card fraud and keep business servers and customer information from being hacked."

"And that's a big deal?" I asked.

"Last year banks wrote off over $25 billion in credit card and identity theft fraud."

"Wait," I said. "That was billion with a *B*?"

"Yup," Hanson answered. "We can't keep the idiots from getting ripped off because they choose lousy passwords, but our software put a damper on in-house theft by making it more difficult for employees to steal information and sell it."

"Okay," I said. "You used your evil hacking skills for good, I get that. But I still don't get the bodyguard."

"Part of the deal was I had to stay on for two years as a consultant. The buyers want me available, so I get a bodyguard. Plus, I can't do any high-risk activities like hang gliding, car racing, or watching cable news shows."

"I'm surprised they let you date Sunny," I said.

"I had to get a waiver," Hanson answered without missing a beat.

"Hey!" Sunny protested.

I always liked a guy who could keep up, and being quick-witted enough to be able to keep Sunny off balance was definitely a point in Hanson's favor.

"So why in the world were you doing an in-home computer repair for my mom?" I asked.

"Believe me," Hanson answered, "it wasn't my idea. I wanted to send one of my guys over, but my mom and your mom were good friends…"

"Really?" I interrupted.

"While we didn't get along in high school, our moms saw so much of each other in four years of us doing many of the same things, they bonded."

"Why?" I demanded.

Hanson sighed. "I think my mom wanted me to be more focused like you and your mom wanted you to be more laid-back like me."

I'm never going to have children.

Hanson continued, "I can't say no to my mother."

"Oh," Sunny said as she rubbed Hanson's cheek. "Such a good son."

"Her computer appeared to have been wiped clean around the time of your visit," I said.

"Guilty as charged," Hanson said. "I encrypted all of her files and put them up on one of my cloud servers."

"Can we get access to them?"

"Sure, but it won't do you any good without her passwords."

"You don't have her passwords?" I asked.

Hanson shook his head. "No. They would've required a reset after the first time your mom logged in. The good news is, most people use the same passwords over and over, so there is a good chance if you can get into her MacBook, you can also get into her cloud account."

"If we can't find the passwords," I asked, "couldn't you just hack into her account?"

Sunny laughed as William grinned at me.

"What?" I protested.

"William got stinkin' rich by writing programs to prevent people from hacking accounts like these."

"She's right," William added. "Plus, even if I accessed the files directly from the server, they would be encrypted, and I would still need the password to read them."

I hate computers.

"But let's not get ahead of ourselves," Hanson continued.

"Meaning?" I asked.

"I have my MacBook in the car. Let's see whether I can get you into your mom's cloud account."

We headed to the parking lot, with William leading the way. When he got to the doorway, he said, "Dammit," and sprinted outside.

CHAPTER TWELVE

I N THE PARKING lot, our idiot cousin was sitting on his butt on the ground, with his back against the rear tire of his car. His eyes were bulging, his face was an even pastier white than normal, and he was gasping for air. Eddie was being tended to by both Dave Davis and Frank Dibble. Harrison, with a blue aluminum bat in his hand, was supervising the proceedings.

"Oh, this is too good," I muttered as I reached for my phone and started videoing.

"What happened?" Hanson demanded as he glared at Harrison.

Harrison shrugged. "As soon as tough guy here got to his car, he pulled this bat out of the trunk of his car and came after me."

"You know I don't like this kind of stuff," Hanson said as his nostrils flared with anger.

"At this moment," Harrison said with a nod in Eddie's direction, "I don't think he likes it much either."

"Is he hurt?"

"Naw," Harrison answered as he tossed the bat toward the opposite end of the parking lot from Eddie's car, where it clattered on the pavement before sliding into the grass.

"Too bad," I muttered, which brought a flicker of a smile to Harrison's face. It vanished as quickly as it had appeared.

"I just knocked the wind out of him," Harrison answered. "For a couple of minutes, he'll think he needs last rites, but then he'll be fine."

Across the lot, Davis and Dibble jumped away from Eddie as he started violently retching, which, thankfully, I caught on my iPhone.

"There's a chance," Harrison added as he glanced over his shoulder at Eddie, "that my little love tap might also cause him to blow his lunch."

When it came to men and my dating habits, I'd always been pretty picky. That put me closer to the prude end than the party girl end of the spectrum. Don't get me wrong, I liked a bit of male companionship just as much as the next girl. But the idea of cruising bars looking to hook up with someone I would never consider marrying, much less having a child with grosses me out. Friends with benefits, ah, no.

I lost my virginity at seventeen, not because I was head over heels in love, but mostly I wanted to see what all the fuss was about. I didn't have the energy or willingness to deal with any potential blowback by being with one of the boys at my high school. Instead I hit it off with a very nice young man I met at a science conference. I thought Timmy was the perfect choice. I was a junior while he was a senior at a nearby school, and he was going away to college in a few months. I assumed that since he was older and male, he would be more worldly; boy, was I wrong. His experience level was exactly the same as mine: zero. He got overheated and started before I was ready, so it hurt a little. Thankfully, it was over quickly. Too quickly for the embarrassed Timmy, whom I never saw or spoke to again after that night.

With that out of my system, it was easy to knuckle down and concentrate on my studies. My next encounter wasn't until my sophomore year of college, when I met Matthew. Matty was sweet and self-effacing when I first met him. The sex was good compared to Timmy, but that wasn't a high bar to get over. We were together nearly a year, but somewhere along the line he morphed into a self-proclaimed social warrior. The longer he stayed on campus, the angrier he became. With me preferring to contract a bad case of malaria to getting involved in politics, we started to drift apart, and our relationship ended with a whimper and not a bang.

Then there was Max — handsome, funny and a holy terror in the boudoir. With him, I learned the true meaning of the word *orgasm*. When he was courting me, he was sweet and attentive. After the conquest, things slowly began to change. Phone calls were not returned. Evenings in replaced going out. The first few times he showed up unannounced with a bottle of red wine and a twinkle in his eye, it was charming. When these booty calls started to be the norm instead of the exception, it got old fast, and I ended the relationship.

My only regret: I never thanked Max for introducing me to Merlot.

Which brought me back to Harrison. He was too old for me, and I doubted an Ivy League humanities major and an ex-military guy would share much common ground. While I would like to credit primal instincts, I was pretty sure fatigue, too much Merlot, and the emotional overload I had experienced today were factors in my present thinking, and that in the morning light, he would be less attractive. But the ease with which Harrison had dispatched my odious cousin, who had terrorized me for two decades, made him, for the moment at least, the sexiest man in the world.

Sunny did a double take when she saw the look on my face, then burst out laughing. "You look like you need a cold shower," she whispered in my ear.

"Shut up."

Sunny leaned in closer. "He's single, you're single, and he is quite the physical specimen. Go for it."

"Shut. Up." I glanced at Harrison and had to agree with Sunny's evaluation, then I forced my eyes back to William, who was opening the trunk of his car.

"What are you two talking about?" William asked.

"Grace wants to shake the trailer with Harrison," Sunny said cheerfully.

William shrugged. "Yeah, he gets that a lot."

I felt my cheeks darkening, and I snuck a quick peek at Harrison, who just smiled at me.

That cold shower was starting to sound pretty damn good.

William closed the trunk, opened his laptop, and placed it on the front hood of his Aston Martin, but its screen was blank. He turned his head sideways so his profile was toward his laptop and hit the enter key. After a few seconds, the computer screen came to life.

"What did you just do?" I asked.

"For the past year or so, I've been working on an ear recognition program using the laptop's built-in camera."

"Really? Ear recognition?" I asked.

"Ears are more unique than fingerprints, and, unlike facial

recognition, ear recognition is not affected by weight gain or loss, or five o'clock shadow."

"Ears?" I repeated.

"If the device doesn't recognize the unique shape and features of your ear," Sunny answered, "it won't allow you access." William and I both gave Sunny an odd look. "What?" she objected. "I only pretend like I'm not paying attention. That way I don't have to talk about boring stuff."

William shook his head, then continued. "Your ears stay pretty much the same from the day you're born until the day you die. Plus, they are on an easily measurable fixed location on the side of your skull, which means even if someone cut your ear off to hack your system, it would be damn near impossible to have it on the exact perfect spot to fool the software."

"Eew," I said squeamishly, realizing how girly I sounded before glancing at Harrison again. Thankfully, he didn't seem to notice or care.

"This is only a prototype," William said. "Once I've got all the bugs out of it, it will make facial recognition obsolete."

"How?"

"Millions of smartphones and computers are stolen every year," William said. "They become a lot less attractive if they're unusable or can't be resold."

"Is that what your company does?"

"Naw." William waved me off. "My company specializes in network security. The ear recognition thing is just a side project I've been tinkering with for a while for my personal amusement." William's fingers danced across the keyboard. "Do you know your mother's password?"

"Capital G-r-a-c-e-Ampersand-Capital S-u-n-n-y exclamation mark-number 1."

William rolled his eyes.

"What?" Sunny demanded. "It has the required capital letter, a special character, and a number."

"If you know it's required, so does every hacker in the world. Since your mom used her two children's names, which a quick search of social media would turn up, it would take the average hacker about two minutes to figure out that password." William's face lit up. "We're in. Thankfully for us, she didn't take my advice on how to make her password unhackable."

"Unhackable?" I asked.

"The English language has roughly two hundred thousand unique words. Select four of them that are easy for you to remember and that have absolutely nothing to do with you; throw in three special characters; string them together like 'Ocean!Dog, Blue&Strong'; and you have a nearly unbeatable password."

"Really?"

"Do the math," William answered. "If the words are truly random, then two hundred thousand times two hundred thousand is forty trillion possible combinations, and that's only for the first two words."

William turned the screen toward Sunny and me. There was a list of folders and files, which were mostly routine things, but the item that caught my eye and immediate interest was a folder titled *MAJIC*.

"That one," I said.

William clicked on it, and a request for a password came up.

"Password protected," William muttered as he typed in *Grace&Sunny!1.* but that didn't work. "Uh oh," William said. He tried it again, but it still didn't work. "Maybe your mom did listen," he said. "If I enter one more bad password, then my security protocols will start to kick in."

"Meaning?" I asked.

"Meaning, after the next failed login, you'll have to wait a minute between attempts. After five failures, it goes to ten minutes between attempts, and after another ten failures, you'll be locked out."

"Why?"

"It prevents a hacker from simply running a computer-based password generation program like Brute Force that keeps trying new combinations." William looked at the file I was trying to open. "What's MAJIC?"

I was in no mood to provide details, but my reluctance didn't seem to slow Sunny down.

"It turns out Mr. MAJIC is Grace's biological father."

"Let me guess," William said. "Your mom was trying to track him down."

"How did you know that?" I asked.

"There weren't any problems with your mom's computer that weren't obviously self-inflicted and easy to repair. She knew I had computer skills, and I suspected my visit was just a ploy to pump me for information. She spent nearly the entire time we were together asking about how she could use the internet to track down someone and was fascinated by my ear recognition program."

I was momentarily stunned.

Mom thought Peterson was still alive and had spent her final days searching for him.

"Did you find him for her?" I asked.

"No. She had seen too many bad TV shows where they run a facial recognition program to find the bad guy and before the next commercial they had him. I told her I had no access to law enforcement databases or the software needed, and wouldn't even know where to start."

I pointed to William's laptop screen. "Can you get us access to this file?"

William sighed. "I can try, but since we're a high-end security company, having one of our own servers getting hacked would be a bit embarrassing."

"Can't you just do a password reset?" Sunny asked.

"No. We have safeguards built into our system that even I can't get around. A reset would still require the original password." William sighed again. "The best I can do is have one of my guys remove the slowdown and lockout feature and try to hack the password."

"How long will that take?" I asked.

William shrugged. "Anywhere from five minutes to fifty years. But without a starting point, and as, ah, interesting as your mother was, I'm guessing it will be closer to fifty years." He shook his head. "I'll do what I can, but you should probably focus your energy on finding the password yourself."

"Do you think she hid it somewhere?" I asked.

"How to put this without sounding cold..."

"Just spit it out," Sunny said, cutting him off.

William drew in a quick breath. "Your mom knew she was dying. If she wanted that file to die with her, all she had to do was delete it from the server, but she didn't." William paused. "I think she wanted it to be found. If that's the case, she would have left the password somewhere for you to find."

"Any suggestions?" Sunny asked.

"Not really," William replied. "The stock answer is to look for it taped under a drawer or in a book that had special meaning, but that would have been risky since someone else might have stumbled on it."

William thought for a few seconds, then snapped his fingers. "When I gave your mom my standard spiel about selecting four words at random and throwing in three special characters, her face lit up, and she said she knew the perfect combination. She said it would be easy for her to remember, and she also said you would be able to figure it out."

CHAPTER THIRTEEN

S UNNY AND I kicked around ideas for a few minutes, and we promised to get back to William with a list of potential words to start from. I thanked Willie — William — for all of his help, and Sunny, being a real trooper, declined William's offer to come home with him to play slap and tickle and stuck with me instead. We also declined an offer of a lift home. While technically a four-seater, the Aston Martin was far from family friendly. While it was tempting to sit in a confined space next to Harrison, there was no elegant way for me to get into the back seat of William's sports car without losing twenty or thirty pounds first.

As we strolled back to our house, Sunny was her usual annoyingly bubbly self.

"I think Harrison likes you."

"How could you tell? The man has the emotional range of the Sphinx."

"Maybe, but I saw the way you looked at him. If it were a felony to undress a man with your eyes, you'd be on your way to supermax."

"Shut. Up. He's not my type."

"Ha! He's a dream come true for every woman with a lick of sense."

"How so?"

"First off, he's an impressive physical specimen who doesn't talk too much," Sunny said as she started warming up to this topic. "Next, he's the kind of guy who would jump out of bed in the middle of the night to check that strange noise without being asked. Most importantly, he's exactly the kind of guy you could build a life around." Sunny drew in a breath, and a small tear formed in the corner of her eye. "We should know."

"Why is that?" I asked.

"Really? You don't see it?"

"See what?" I objected.

"Harrison and Daddy are cut from the same bolt of cloth."

This stopped me dead in my tracks.

Sunny was right.

I took two quick steps to catch back up, but Sunny's observation had left me at a loss for words. We walked along in silence for half a block, and when we rounded the corner where we could see our house, Sunny pointed to our front porch. There were two men, one of them obviously Dad, sitting on the stoop; I had no idea who the other man might be. As we got closer, we could see Dad was talking to a fit elderly man, probably around seventy, with a headful of snow white hair.

Dad was in the early to bed and early rise school of thought and the idea of him drinking on our porch after midnight with someone I was certain I had never seen before was considerably more than unusual.

When the duo saw us approaching, they both put down their beer bottles and rose to their feet. The old guy clearly had either seen my picture before or had been given a very good description. He walked straight up to me and extended his hand.

"I'm John Cutter," he said in a deep baritone. "Mark Franklin sent me."

I accepted his hand. His grip was dry and firm but not aggressive.

"You certainly got here quickly enough."

"I've been chasing Mr. MAJIC for over twenty years now, ma'am," Cutter said while making excellent eye contact. "When Mr. Franklin told me what you had, I jumped in my car and drove straight here." Cutter nodded at Sunny. "If it wouldn't be too much bother, would it be possible for me to see the manuscript?"

"Sure," I answered.

Cutter gathered up a battered old briefcase as Sunny led the way into the house with Dad and me taking up the rear.

Dad grabbed my arm to slow me down. "A heads up that he was coming and maybe a note where you two were off to would have been nice," Dad said softly. "Since I had no idea who this guy was, I wasn't going to let him in the house."

"Sorry," I answered. "You were already in bed, and I didn't expect him to get here in the middle of the night."

"Where'd you two go?"

"The Pub to talk to Sunny's boyfriend."

"The one with the drug-dealer car and the bodyguard?"

"Yeah"

"Great," Dad said. "Nothing like both my daughters traipsing off to a bar at midnight to see the younger one's sketchy boyfriend."

"Sketchy," I said with a laugh. "You don't know William at all, do you?"

Dad shrugged.

"He was unwinding from the megadollar sale of one of his internet security companies by sitting in with the band." I smiled so broadly my jaw hurt.

"What else?" Dad was suspicious of my smile, and rightly so.

"Cousin Eddie was there and mouthing off to Sunny and me."

"Surprise, surprise."

"Eddie was about to slap Sunny…"

"What?" Dad said as he was now fully awake and had fire in his eyes. I had a feeling the next time Dad and Eddie crossed paths, it would not end well for my plump cousin.

"Relax," I said as I gave his arm a squeeze. "William's bodyguard showed him the error of his ways, then Eddie was stupid enough to go after him with a baseball bat in the parking lot." I played the video, and when it got to the place where Eddie threw up, Dad burst out laughing.

"I want to buy this guy a beer."

"If I see him again, I'll let him know," I said as we caught up with Sunny and John Cutter in Mom's office. Cutter was already at the desk thumbing through the manuscript.

"Do you have the envelope it was in?" Cutter asked.

I grabbed the envelope, which was next to Mom's printer, and handed it to him.

Cutter looked at the envelope and focused most of his attention on the cellophane tape. "Was there anything else in the envelope?"

"A golden straw," Sunny said.

"Excuse me?" Cutter asked.

"It's a long story and has nothing to do with Peterson," I answered. "I have it up on the nightstand next to my bed if you need to see it."

"That's not necessary at the moment," Cutter answered as he continued examining the envelope and manuscript. "It looks to be the right age, and Mr. Franklin said he was convinced it was written by Mr. MAJIC."

"Yeah, but how do we prove it?" I asked.

"I understand there was a note from your mother claiming Simon Alphonse Peterson was your natural father?"

"It's also upstairs in my room. I'll go get it." As I turned to head for the door, Cutter stopped me.

"That won't be necessary," Cutter said as he continued to flip through the manuscript. He repeated what I had done earlier by turning the paper over to see whether the ink had penetrated. This didn't escape the attention of Sunny, who glanced at me and nodded her approval. "That note won't help your paternity case one bit."

"Why not?" I asked.

"Because Simon Alphonse Peterson is not your biological father."

"You say that with a lot of confidence," Sunny said. "How can you be so sure?"

Cutter glanced up at me. "Simon Alphonse Peterson died fifty-seven years ago."

CHAPTER FOURTEEN

"I blinked three times, then said, "Excuse me?"

"The real Simon Alphonse Peterson died in Little Rock, Arkansas. His parents were involved in an automobile accident when his mother was over eight months pregnant. The father died at the scene of the crash, but the mother lived long enough for a Caesarian birth before succumbing to her injuries. The boy died three days later."

A stunned silence settled over the room.

Finally, I broke the spell. "Then who was the person claiming to be Peterson?"

Cutter laughed. "That's the question I've been trying to answer for the past twenty-four years."

"Hold on, hold on," Sunny said as she checked her phone. "I've done some research on Peterson, and there was no mention that he was an identity thief."

"I may be the only person in the world to have figured it out," Cutter said.

"And you can prove this?" I asked.

Cutter pulled an iPad mini out of his briefcase and tapped a few keys, then turned the screen to where Sunny and I could see it. It was a pdf of the death certificate of Simon Alphonse Peterson. "I have certified copies of both his birth and death certificates in my safe deposit box."

"I still find this hard to believe," Sunny said.

"It was a long con, and this guy was good — I mean, really good. He probably spent months looking for the perfect cover."

"Perfect? How so?" I asked.

"He needed someone around his age who had died very young, with both parents dead and no traceable next of kin. With that combination, the odds anyone would recognize the name were minimal. From there it was easy enough to get a birth certificate, which he used to get a Social Security number and began building a history." Cutter shook his head. "Unless you knew where to look, for all intents and purposes, Simon Alphonse Peterson was very much alive. His paper trail indicated he owned a car, had a job, and paid his taxes. It was a near CIA level false ID."

"CIA?" I said with a startled expression on my face. "Are you saying this guy was some kind of spy?"

"No," Cutter said with a dismissive wave of his hand. "The CIA would have gotten rid of the death certificate. He was just a very well-organized con man who was willing to do the necessary groundwork that would allow him to disappear when the time was right, without leaving a trace."

"Okay," Sunny said, "I'm confused. If his paper trail indicated he was real, why did you bother to look so much deeper than anyone else?"

"As the lead detective on his disappearance, I was much closer to the investigation than anyone else, and I saw a pattern no one else noticed," Cutter said. "Peterson was only around on weekends. In the four years while he was at the zenith of his popularity, I could not confirm any sighting of him on a weekday. He was only seen at his weekend seminars and never anyplace else. He had a Manhattan co-op, but when we investigated it, we couldn't find a single person, including the doorman, who could remember ever seeing him, and when we finally convinced a judge to let us search it for a possible body, it looked like it had never been lived in. Plus, especially after he vanished, it was clear why he dressed the way he did, banned recording devices in the audience of his shows, and avoided cameras as much as possible; he was trying to hide his true identity. This made me curious. After I retired, I made a trip to Little Rock and discovered the truth."

"Wow!" I said. "He certainly went to a lot of trouble."

"Agreed," Cutter answered. "Which was really odd, considering none of this was necessary."

Cutter noticed the puzzled expression on my face and continued, "While a mountain of cash vanished with him, he did absolutely nothing illegal. This guy claiming to be Peterson had no bogus life insurance policies for anyone to collect on. He paid all his income taxes. Before he liquidated all of his assets and converted them to cash, everything he owned was paid for in full, with no mortgages, so there was no bank fraud. He even left enough money in the account to give all of his employees six months of severance pay."

"Isn't ID theft itself a crime?" Sunny asked.

"Possibly," Cutter answered with a chuckle. "But, he didn't steal a valid Social Security number and open up fake accounts. Since no one was injured, no one had standing to file civil charges. Even if we had tried to pursue that line of investigation as criminal, Mr. MAJIC Inc. had filed a DBA…"

Sunny saw the blank look on my face and added, "Doing Business As."

"Right," Cutter said. "Then they registered a FBN for S.A. Peterson." Cutter glanced at me then added, "Fictitious Business Name."

"That's brilliant," Sunny said with a laugh. "That made them legally bulletproof."

"How so?" I demanded.

Sunny shrugged. "Going after MAJIC Inc. for Peterson would be like going after McDonald's for Ronald McDonald. S.A. Peterson was just a fictitious front man, and they had registered documents to prove it." Sunny shook her head. "What I don't understand is: Why go to all of that trouble if he wasn't doing anything illegal?"

"When I find him, I'll ask."

"So, you think he's still alive?" Sunny asked.

"I have no reason to think otherwise and I'm guessing he is pretty close to the same age as the real Peterson," Cutter answered. "That would mean he is only in his mid – to late fifties." Cutter sighed. "If you really want to know whether the man your mother thought was Peterson is your father, I can help with that."

"How?" I asked.

Cutter reached into his briefcase and pulled out an old photograph. "MAJIC was completely anal about being photographed; this is one of the few photos of him in existence. Everyone thought he was just being quirky until he vanished."

The black and white photo was the same one that was attached to the "What Ever Happened to Mr. MAJIC?" article from *Rolling Stone* magazine. This one was the original, so the quality was much better than the print halftone I had seen earlier. Peterson was putting his hand up to block the lens, but he had been too slow in reacting to prevent the shot. He had a dark, shaggy wig and was wearing oversized sunglasses.

"MAJIC was seldom seen in public and was never seen anywhere without his hairpiece or sunglasses," Cutter said. "I later realized this was another of his clever tricks he learned from Groucho Marx."

"Who?" Sunny asked.

"Jesus," Cutter muttered. "He was one of the famous Marx Brothers. He had a greasepaint moustache and eyebrows. Even though he was probably the most recognizable man in the world while in make-up, without his make-up on, he could be sitting next to you in a restaurant and you'd never notice. The same was true for MAJIC."

Sunny Googled Groucho and nodded at his picture. "Oh, I've seen him before."

"This is all very interesting," I said, "but how does any of this prove paternity?"

"I came into possession of one of his hairpieces, and inside I found a hair that still had its follicle. From that I was able to get a full DNA profile of the man claiming to be Peterson."

I felt a tingle go up my spine.

"But," Cutter added, "while it will satisfy you, me, and maybe even Nathaniel Goodman, it would never satisfy a judge enough to get you declared his daughter."

Sunny giggled. "Oh, you dog," she said. "Let me guess; there might be a chain of custody issue."

Cutter pointed to Sunny and grinned. "Bingo."

"Okay. What does that mean?" I asked.

"It means he stole the wig from the evidence locker, so legally, the DNA is considered tainted and inadmissible in a court of law."

"Franklin warned me about you," Cutter said. "Actually, since the hairpiece was mailed to us anonymously, and we had no way to prove its authenticity, it was never considered evidence."

"How did you end up with it?" I asked.

"When the case went stone cold, I got permission to take it as a retirement gift."

"Retirement?"

"Peterson was my last case."

"What happened?" Sunny asked.

"Since the guy claiming to be Peterson went MIA in Manhattan, and it was a high-profile case, this hot potato ended up in my lap in the Major Crimes Division. What should have been a routine missing-person case turned into a seemingly never-ending media circus. When we came up empty, guess who they blamed?"

"Victory has a thousand fathers, but defeat is an orphan," I said.

Cutter nodded. "Despite no evidence or leads, I worked the Peterson case for two months before the department ordered me to move on. Then suggested, after all of the bad press, I take my retirement."

"Ah," I said. "That explains your Captain Ahab complex."

"Forgive my sister, she's a literature major," Sunny said with a grin aimed directly at me.

Cutter laughed. "Never thought of it like that. I guess MAJIC is my Moby Dick." Cutter put his hand over a yawn. "This is the first fresh lead I've had in a while and the first time I've felt like I'm earning my retainer."

"Retainer?" I asked.

"Nathaniel Goodman has been bankrolling all of my investigations for years."

"Why?" Sunny asked.

"With Goodman it's hard to say. It could be because he misses his old friend or because he felt bad that Peterson cost me my job or because he wants me to find Peterson so he can punch the son-of-bitch in the nose."

Sunny's eyes unfocused, which meant her mind had just kicked into overdrive, then she refocused and she smiled. "Or," she said, "it could just be a good business investment." Sunny saw the puzzled expression on all of our faces and continued, "The Peterson books are the goose that lays the golden eggs for his little vanity publishing house. He may be willing to pay Mr. Cutter here a retainer just so he has no surprises when it comes to Peterson." Sunny turned to Cutter. "When you discovered Peterson was fake, why didn't you tell anyone?"

Cutter could see where this was going and nodded his approval. "Because Nathaniel Goodman asked me to keep it to myself."

"If this is such a secret," Sunny said mischievously, "why are you telling this to us?"

"Because Mr. Goodman told me to."

We spent the next few minutes exploring possibilities until we had a simultaneous epiphany: We were all too tired to form any rational conclusions, so we should call it a night. Instead of Cutter trying to find a motel room at two in the morning, Dad offered him the living room couch, which he accepted.

CHAPTER FIFTEEN

OTHER THAN NOT being a big fan of pasta, my dad has never been picky about his food or drink — except when it comes to his morning coffee. He likes it strong, black, and in large quantities. With him being an early riser, and my bedroom being directly over the kitchen, the smell of coffee brewing in the morning always triggers a cascade of childhood memories for me. Mom and Sunny were slow starters, so I was usually the second one downstairs in the morning. After getting in my chair, I always got a smile, a soft shoulder squeeze, and a kiss on the back of my head. By the time I turned fourteen, he had me hooked on French dark roast and convinced that adding cream or sugar was a sign of personal weakness.

My eyes fluttered open at the familiar smell of Dad's coffee, and I quickly threw on some clothes and headed downstairs. Sitting in my usual chair at the four-seat kitchen table, cradling a large mug of coffee, was John Cutter. He looked like he could have used a few more hours of sleep and was badly in need of a shave. He nodded in my direction when I came in. Dad, hearing me coming down the stairs, had my favorite mug with *Hello Darkness, My Old Friend* printed on the side filled and waiting for me on the kitchen counter. As I reached for it, I felt a soft squeeze on my shoulder and felt a kiss on the back of my head.

Home.

I couldn't quite bring myself to sit in Dad's or Sunny's usual spot at the table, let alone take Mom's seat. I leaned against the sink instead. "So," I said to Cutter, "any suggestions on where we start?"

"Let's start with a step-by-step recount of everything you've done since you got here."

"That's sounds like a waste of time."

"Humor me," Cutter said. "Ninety-nine percent of investigating is a waste of time. But one hundred percent of being a good investigator is figuring out the one percent that is important."

Not wanting to be a part of this discussion, and also not wanting to make a scene in front of our guest, Dad quietly left Cutter and me alone. I spent the next twenty minutes telling Cutter about the letter from the lawyer, the manuscript in Mom's magic box, and the files Sunny's boyfriend put on the cloud that we were trying to open.

After I was finished, he asked a few questions to be sure he understood exactly what had happened and had me repeat the part about using four unrelated — but easily remembered — words plus three special characters as an unbreakable password. His poker face was better than most, but it was easy to tell he didn't like what he heard.

Then he asked to see the business card of the lawyer, which he photographed with his smart phone, then sent a copy of it off somewhere. Next he wanted to see the box the manuscript had been in. It was up in Sunny's room, but Cutter said it wasn't urgent, so we decided to wait until my sister got up instead of disturbing her beauty sleep. Then he suggested we adjourn to Mom's office for a closer look around.

Cutter stopped in the doorway of the office, and his old-school cop training kicked in. His eyes slowly and systematically took in the entire room. It was like he was working a grid and wanted to be sure he didn't overlook any detail. "Do you mind if I make a bit of a mess?" he asked politely.

"Knock yourself out," I answered. "What are you looking for?"

"There is a slim chance your mom wrote her cloud password down and hid it somewhere in here."

"Okay," I said. "But if she took William's advice about four words that were easy to remember, then she probably wouldn't need to write it down."

"Agreed," Cutter answered. "But remember, ninety-nine percent of investigating is a waste of time. I want to do my due diligence and hit the high spots people use to hide passwords — taped to the bottom of drawers, under lamps."

"What are the odds that you'll find it?"

Cutter shrugged. "I'd say close to zero. This is a fair-sized house with a couple of outbuildings, and we're looking for a slip of paper that could fit in a fortune cookie. I could bring in a top forensics team, and they could spend a week here and never find it."

"How can I help?"

"We know your mom hired an attorney and he used your sister's boyfriend for help. See whether you can find her bank records, and see whether there are any other unusual expenses."

Clearly Mr. Franklin had made the right choice in sending Cutter here to do the sleuthing. Despite years of immersing myself in crime novels, I was at a complete loss for where to begin on any of this, including the relatively simple task of looking for Mom's bank records. Did she have printed statements? If yes, where were they, and how many months did she keep? Did she do online banking — which would mean figuring out which bank, user name, and password she'd used?

Yikes!

Before complete panic mode set in, Sunny, with her hair pulled back in a ponytail and wearing red flannel, one-piece footed pajamas that made her look twelve, wandered in. "What's up?" she asked as she made no effort to cover her oversized yawn.

"Any idea where Mom kept her bank records?"

Sunny turned her head in the direction of the kitchen and yelled, "Dad! Where did Mom keep her bank statements?"

From somewhere deep within the bowels of the house came the reply. "Bottom right hand desk drawer."

"Bottom right hand desk drawer," Sunny repeated as she turned blurry-eyed toward the kitchen. "Coffee," she said as she disappeared as quickly as she had arrived.

I opened the drawer and found a hanging file that was packed with oversized brightly colored file folders containing tax records and every bank statement for my family since, apparently, before Watergate. I knew Mom's workshop was a nightmare, but I had no idea her hoarder instincts included a twenty-year-old receipt from OfficeMax for a ream of typing paper. At the front of the row was a big yellow oversized hanging folder with a plastic thingy on top that said *Banking*. It contained over a dozen manila file folders, each marked with a year on the tab.

I pulled out the one for this year and started thumbing through it. There was nothing of interest until I got four months back and saw a familiar name: Wilson Prentice, attorney-at-law. The check Mom had cut was much larger than I would have expected to deliver a simple graveside notification and was an odd amount. I was just about to say something to Cutter when I noticed the next statement down from the previous month also had a smaller debit to Prentice for exactly $1,000. I thumbed back through the rest of the years, and nothing else popped out.

"What do you make of this?" I asked Cutter as I handed him the statements.

Cutter looked at them, then laid them side by side on the desktop. "This earlier one, since it is an even dollar amount, was probably a retainer."

"What about the second one?"

"Clearly," Cutter said, "Prentice did some billable work for your mother. See whether there is an itemized statement in the drawer."

Why didn't I think of that? Miss Marple, I ain't.

With Mom's well-organized filing system, it only took me a few seconds to find the bill from Prentice. "All it says is 'for services rendered.'" I handed the statement to Cutter. "What does that mean?"

"Hard to say. It could have been for a will or probate work," Cutter answered. His phone beeped, and he read the message. "It looks like the honorable Wilson Prentice is one of those anything-for-a-buck one-man shops that handles stuff from slip-and-fall litigation to DWI defense."

"Why would my mom hire a guy like that?"

"One way to find out is to ask him." Cutter found his office hours on the report. "He won't be in for a few hours."

"Who won't be in for a few hours?" Sunny asked as she glided into Mom's office cradling her coffee mug in both hands.

"That attorney from the funeral yesterday," I answered. "According to Mom's bank records, he was doing more for her than just delivering graveside notes."

"That should give us all time to get cleaned up," Sunny said as she blew on her mug of coffee.

"Who is this 'us' you're referring to?" I asked.

"Me, you, and Mr. Detective Man," Sunny said brightly as she tried her coffee but it was still too hot. "If you think I'm going to miss any of this, you're nuts."

CHAPTER SIXTEEN

S TARING AT THE mirror, I was glad I had let Sunny take the first shower. Our entire lives, she had never needed more than ten minutes in the bathroom we shared to look fabulous. She didn't hog the hot water, and she was usually in and out so fast the mirror didn't even have time to steam up. As a kid, since I had to work twice as hard to look half as good, I resented her grooming habits; now, with my rapidly improving opinion of her, I was just jealous.

I hadn't slept well; too much was swirling around in my head for me to unwind, and it showed. The face staring back at me in the mirror was tired, and its eyes were slightly bloodshot. The second mug of Dad's excellent coffee was helping me shake out the cobwebs, but the best I could do for my appearance was triage. I started by fishing eye drops out of my make-up kit, which took care of my bloodshot eyes but the rest would require major surgery, which would have to wait.

Dad was alone in the kitchen when I entered. "Where's the dynamic duo?" I asked as I headed to the coffee maker for round three. Sunny had raided the refrigerator, and an assortment of casseroles and cheese trays were on the kitchen table. They hadn't looked appetizing the night before, and their appeal hadn't improved with age.

"Cutter wanted to have a look at your mom's workshop. Sunny is giving him the grand tour."

I gave the food on the table a second look and quickly moved on.

"Do you know anything about the money Mom paid that attorney guy?"

Dad gave me an odd look before he answered. "I know she paid him, but she never told me why, and I never asked." His tone was stiff and measured.

"It was a pretty good chunk of money," I said. "Weren't you curious?"

Dad sighed, then stepped around me to start another pot of coffee.

"I knew it had something to do with Simon Peterson, and that was all I needed or wanted to know."

"I was just…"

"Stop, Grace," he snapped, realized what he had done, then immediately softened his tone. "Please just stop."

His eyes locked on the backyard through the kitchen window as he leaned on the sink. "I understand your desire to find Peterson. I get that, I really do. But your mother and I always had an understanding that we would never talk about Peterson, and I would really appreciate it if you would show me the same courtesy." Dad picked up a towel and dried his hands and threw the towel on the counter before wheeling to face me. "Just leave me out of it, okay?"

"Daddy, I didn't…"

He wasn't listening; he was already heading out of the room.

Crap.

I took a step toward the door to follow him but stopped. Even if I caught up to him, what was I going to say? Mom had left me the manuscript for a reason. While obviously curious, I harbored no unquenchable desire to find or meet my biological father — but there was just too much at stake to walk away.

While I was lost in my thoughts, I didn't hear Sunny and Cutter enter the kitchen.

"You ready to roll?" Sunny asked, then she saw the look on my face. "What happened?"

"Dad yelled at me."

"Really? He never yells."

"He made it clear he would rather not hear any more about Peterson."

"That's another one of those tough things about having relationships with power over you, especially the good ones."

"Please, Sunny, none of your New Age nonsense right now."

"I'm just saying, when you have a choice, you need to do what is right for you and not worry about how it affects anyone else."

"That's pretty cold," I said.

"From your perspective, maybe. From mine, why make yourself miserable trying to please someone else? Especially when there is a very good chance, even if you bend completely to their will, it won't ever be enough to satisfy them. As soon as they see they have power over you, they will constantly move the goal post and make it a no-win situation for you. You can get into an endless downward spiral where they have more and more power over you. We all have to find our own path to happiness, and sometimes that creates conflict."

"Are you done?"

"Almost," Sunny said brightly. "Grace, you love Dad, and he loves you. Neither one of you wants to hurt the other, but sweetie, you are now officially on a personal vision quest that, for good or bad, will change you forever. You've spent your entire life getting ready for this moment. Don't let Dad or me or Mom or even Mr. Cutter here cause you to stop doing what you know in your heart of hearts is right for you." Sunny smiled sweetly. "Okay, now I'm done."

John Cutter was looking at Sunny with a stunned, open-mouthed expression on his face as if he were trying to figure out what alien galaxy she had just beamed in from. He blinked a couple of times, shook his head, and turned his attention to me. "Do you have access to your mom's hairbrush?" Cutter asked.

"Sure," I answered with a shrug. "Why?"

"Our first stop will be the attorney's office, then we'll need to find a place where we can do a DNA profile run on both you and your mother to compare to the sample I have from Mr. MAJIC."

***

I had rented the smallest and cheapest car I could find. Since Sunny's car was on its last legs and had an unnerving death rattle every time she turned it off, we opted to ride in Cutter's ancient Crown Vic. I rode shotgun, and Sunny took the backseat. The office of Wilson Prentice, attorney-at-law, was in a small strip mall that was showing its age. It was between a Skyline Chili restaurant and a storefront that had multiple *For Rent* signs in the window. With it being too early for lunch, the heavily pot-holed parking lot was nearly empty.

Cutter weaved between the worst of the road hazards, and, since the lot's parking spaces hadn't been restriped since before I was in kindergarten, he made a best guess and pulled into an open space in front of Prentice's office.

The interior of the office wasn't any more impressive than the exterior. There was an empty desk where a receptionist would sit, if he ever actually needed to hire one, and a half dozen mismatched chairs.

"What a dump," I muttered.

"I've seen worse," Cutter replied.

I didn't doubt that for one moment.

Prentice, hearing the exterior door open, popped his head out of his office. "Ms. Maxwell. I've been expecting you."

"You were?"

"Yes, indeed," Prentice answered cheerfully. "Your mother said it was likely you would show up within a few days after I delivered her letter."

"She did?"

"That is so Mom," Sunny muttered to herself.

Prentice briefly glanced at Sunny, and then his eyes locked on Cutter. "I recognize your sister from yesterday but not your companion. Has this become a police matter?"

"He's NYPD Detective John Cutter," I answered.

"Retired," Cutter added as he showed Prentice his private investigator's license.

Prentice glanced at Cutter's ID. I got the impression Prentice was the kind of lawyer that had crossed paths with more than his share of private investigators and police officers before. If he were a character in one of my hard-boiled novels, his client list would also include hookers and gun molls, along with drug dealers and loan sharks.

"Please come into my office," Prentice said. "I have another letter for you."

CHAPTER SEVENTEEN

PRENTICE'S OFFICE HAD only two chairs in front of the battered old desk, and Cutter waved off the offer of pulling up a third and instead leaned against a credenza. Locating his reading glasses and placing them on his nose, Prentice moved to the opposite side of the desk from Sunny and me and thumbed through a stack of papers.

"Ah, here we are," Prentice said as he slid a sealed nine-by-twelve white envelope across the desk to a spot in front of me.

With me being an embarrassing bust at sleuthing so far, on the drive over I had used all of my hard-boiled moxie to make a mental list of the questions I wanted to ask Prentice. I had even settled on being the alluringly sophisticated damsel in distress who, instead of asking Sam Spade for his help in finding the Maltese Falcon, wanted to know what "services" he had rendered to justify the check my mom had written. I planned to keep Prentice off balance with my quick wit and lively banter. I had even undone an extra button on my blouse to, hopefully, distract him. With the jaw-dropping Sunny sitting next to me, I knew that the extra button thing was a bit of a reach, but a girl can dream.

All of my careful preparations faded away as my eyes locked on the handwritten word, *Grace*, on the outside of the envelope. I glanced at Sunny, who, without taking her eyes off the envelope, was doing the breathing exercise she had taught me. That seemed like a good idea; I joined her.

Feeling a bit better, I reached for the envelope and opened it. The first thing that struck me as odd was that the contents were printed and not handwritten. Mom thought word processing was cold and impersonal and preferred the touch of the paper and the feel of the pen in her hand when crafting her messages. Obviously, this was something different. My immediate guess was this was a document she had worked on for a long period of time, revising and editing it to be sure she got every word exactly right. As soon as I started reading, my suspicion was confirmed.

Grace:

Where to begin. I'm sure you've been told this many times, but I also doubt you would have believed it, but I was very much like you in my adolescent years. I was in pain and confused and, like you, searching for the meaning of life and trying to find my place in this world.

On one level, you were luckier than I; early on, you found a safe place in your books, which allowed you to fold into yourself and find some measure of peace. In college I majored in philosophy, which generated more questions than answers for me.

My four years at Berkeley tracked perfectly with the rise and fall of S.A. Peterson. I found his first two books borderline interesting, but early in my senior year, his third book came out. It was initially so popular, the campus bookstore had trouble keeping it in stock. It became the cool accessory to carry around to impress your classmates with your depth and seriousness.

I thought it was tripe. I read it and found it to be the same mishmash of philosophy and religious tenets of his first two books but had nothing new to say from the earlier tomes. It was like he had melded all of the important life lessons we needed to be happy, updated the archaic language, and then condensed them down to an easy-to-understand philosophy written by psychologists and marketing people, all composed at an eighth-grade comprehension level.

God is in all of us and all things.

You intuitively already know what is right for you.

Don't let others control you.

Love yourself and love others and you will find divine happiness.

Blah, blah, blah.

He had, in my opinion, basically plagiarized and repackaged the historical insights of the ages.

Curious, I attended one of his events in San Francisco and, while his basic premise was unrefined, I was impressed with Peterson's grasp of showmanship. He used all the tools and gimmicks to whip the crowd into a frenzy. I saw grown men weeping and women acting as if they were teenagers at a teen idol rock concert; the energy in the room was astounding.

During his presentation, he discussed some interesting relaxation and releasing techniques I had never heard of before. Later that night, still a bit pumped up from the energy in the room, I tried the techniques and was stunned by what happened. After having the worst nightmare of my life, I awoke with a new understanding and new clarity.

I was a completely different person, and I had Mr. MAJIC to thank. So I did.

I spent the next three days writing a detailed critique of his event and his books and how they had affected me. I also offered some suggestions of how he could modify his seminars so others could experience the same thing I had. Feeling like a new woman, and with that off of my chest, I dropped the letter in the mail and got on with my life. Much to my surprise, he wrote back.

We spent the next few months exchanging letters and thoughts. Then he did the most remarkable thing; he hired me to help him to write his next book. He wanted me to be a role model and use his popularity to actually make a difference in people's lives.

He sent me a terrible first draft of The True Path of Enlightenment, which I eviscerated. Instead of dismissing me as a know-nothing college kid — as I expected — he took all of my comments to heart. We spent the next several months exchanging notes and drafts, oddly, without ever meeting face-to-face or even speaking on the phone. We dealt with each other exclusively via the written word, but I had never felt closer to anyone in my entire life.

As we neared completion of the manuscript, Peterson was doing one of his gala seminars in Silicon Valley and invited me to meet him after the event. Without going into too much detail, with my judgment clouded by a bit too much wine, we ended up creating you.

Six weeks later, when I realized I was pregnant, I traveled to New York to speak to Peterson in person and deliver the latest draft of the manuscript. I talked my way into his hotel room at the event. I arrived while he was showering to get ready to go on stage, and I was shocked by what I found. First, I discovered a set of documents compiled by a private investigator outlining sexual abuse and drug usage by Peterson's staff and the potential for multiple lawsuits if action wasn't taken. The details of the report were disgusting and would have made Caligula blush. I was horrified.

Then there was the hairpiece. I didn't think anything of it until Peterson stepped out of the bathroom and he was unrecognizable without his stage make-up.

Confused and hurt, I grabbed the wig, the stack of investigative reports and the manuscript we had worked on together and fled the room. I sent Peterson a message telling him if he ever contacted me again, I would release the dossier exposing him as a fraud and destroy his empire.

I did not tell him about you, and I never heard from him again.

That very night, S.A. Peterson didn't show up for his event, and the next day, the reports of his disappearance became headline news.

I realized what a mess I had made of my life and knew I had options, but I couldn't bring myself to exercise the most extreme one. Instead I returned home, and thankfully, my rock-solid Don was ready, willing and able to take me back, even in my condition.

Don loved you as if you were his own.

When I learned the authorities were searching for Peterson, I mailed the hairpiece and copy of the private investigator's file to the New York Police Department, then got on with my life and never looked back.

*Grace, please read the manuscript. I hope and pray it will lead
you to the inner peace it has given me.*
Peace Love & Joy Always,
Mom

I handed the letter to Sunny and turned my attention to the next
thing that had been in the envelope. It was the detective report Mom
had mentioned in the letter.

"Well," Sunny said as she glanced at Cutter. "At least now we know
where the hairpiece came from."

That got John Cutter's attention. "May I?" he asked tentatively.

I drew in a cleansing breath, then nodded to Sunny, who handed it
to him.

After he finished reading it, Cutter shook his head and said, "This
ties up a lot of loose ends. Only a handful of people knew about the
dossier, and its existence was never made public."

"You mean this?" I asked Cutter as I handed him the stack of
yellowing pages.

Cutter's eyes grew large as he quickly thumbed through to the last
page, which contained the signature of the investigator. "Sweet Jesus,"
he muttered. His cheeks darkened slightly as he ran his finger over
the raised impression made by the embossing notary seal. He held the
page up to the light, and even from where I was standing, I could see
the ink from the signature had bled through. "I was working from a
photocopy," Cutter said. "This is the original document." His hand
quivered as he reached for his cellphone.

"Who are you calling?" Sunny asked

"Nathaniel Goodman."

"Why?" I demanded.

"To let him know..." His eyes locked on mine. "That I've found
S.A. Peterson's biological daughter."

CHAPTER EIGHTEEN

J OHN CUTTER STEPPED outside the office to place his call. As I finished reading each page of the dossier the private investigator had produced twenty-four years ago, I passed it over to Sunny.

A rare frown covered Sunny's face. "If half of this is true, then I can understand why Peterson took a powder."

"That was only the tip of the iceberg," Cutter said as he reentered the office. "The people surrounding Peterson were some seriously amoral scumbags. Unfortunately, we were never able to make a case against anyone."

"Why not?" I asked.

"Let me guess," Sunny said, "Peterson bought everybody off."

"It wasn't necessary," Cutter answered. "His staff lawyered up, and any and all potential witnesses either refused to testify or were outside of the NYPD jurisdiction. We ran into one embarrassing, and well-publicized, dead end after another. The New York City tabloids were having a field day." Cutter shook his head. "With each new headline, the pressure on me and my team got worse and worse. I think the mayor and the police commissioner both had me on their speed dial. But in terms of the investigation, we had no evidence of foul play, and no one with standing even filed a missing-person report. We only had unsubstantiated hearsay, which was inadmissible."

"So everyone just walked?" I asked incredulously.

"It was one of those victimless crimes," Cutter answered. "We couldn't prove the drug abuse, and none of the Peterson groupies were complaining. If anything, they were proud of what they had done, so we were stuck."

"I thought he cleaned out all of the bank accounts when he vanished. Wasn't that enough to empanel a grand jury?"

"He did clean out his bank accounts," Cutter answered. "But, as his lawyers so eloquently pointed out to us, it was his money, earned legally and with all the taxes paid, so he could do what he wanted to with it, and we could essentially go fly a kite. Whenever we tried to get search warrants, with no evidence of a crime or probable cause that Peterson was involved, we got laughed out of court."

Wilson Prentice cleared his throat. I had forgotten he was even in the room. I gathered up all the papers and placed them back in the envelope before turning my attention back to the lawyer. "Are you holding any more letters from my mother?" I asked bluntly.

"No," Prentice answered.

"My mother paid you a rather large sum of money, and your invoice only stated it was for service rendered. Can you please provide a more itemized accounting?"

Prentice smiled. "You mother predicted you would make that very request, and she was correct." Prentice opened a file drawer and produced a single sheet of paper listing all expenses. My eyes scanned the statement and fixed on a single name that had received the bulk of the money. "Who is Frank Taranto?" I asked.

"Your mother requested I recommend a private investigator for her to help her locate someone, and I secured the services of Mr. Taranto for her. He specializes in finding missing persons." Prentice slid Taranto's card across the desk and in front of me but Cutter intercepted it, took a picture of it with his phone, attached it to a message, and sent the image somewhere.

John Cutter snorted as he looked at the card. "Let me guess, most of these missing persons Taranto finds are bail-bond skips and deadbeat dads behind on their child support."

Wilson Prentice shrugged but didn't answer.

I shook my head and turned my attention back to Prentice. "Did this Frank Taranto have any success?" I asked.

"That I do not know," Prentice answered. "Neither he nor your mother felt compelled to keep me informed of the scope of the investigation nor the details of the results."

"Where can I get a paternity DNA profile done right and done today, if I don't care what it costs?"

"Does it need to stand up in court?"

"No," Cutter answered. "It's a simple comparison for our own personal information."

Prentice pulled another business card out of his drawer for a testing lab. "I assume it is for Ms. Maxwell?"

"Yes," Cutter answered.

"Do you have a sample from the suspected father?"

"I already have the printed results."

Prentice shook his head and muttered, "Remarkable woman." Prentice turned to me. "Your mother anticipated you would want a paternity test. This lab should have her DNA test results on file."

So much for needing the hairbrush.

"That's where you referred her?" I asked.

"The other way around," Prentice answered. "She had the DNA test done first."

Sunny and I exchanged glances and nodded. We both figured she knew she was going to need a DNA profile to prove paternity and went to the lab closest to our house first and they sent her here. That explained how she ended up with a bottom feeder like Prentice for her attorney.

"Where is the lab?" I asked.

"It is two blocks down the street on the left hand side. For the right price, they can give you a four-hour turnaround. Ask for Lenny."

"How much is the right price?" Cutter asked.

Prentice eyed Cutter, then said, "Lenny will ask for two grand but settle for fifteen hundred."

Cutter put both hands on the desk and leaned across to get nose to nose with Prentice. "Is there anything you're holding back that Grace should know?"

Prentice leaned back so Cutter was no longer in his personal space and shook his head.

Cutter reached into his pocket and peeled off a one-hundred-dollar bill from a wad bigger than his fist and laid the C-note in front of Prentice with his hand over it.

"Are you sure?"

Prentice eyed the cash and slowly licked his lips. "Elizabeth Maxwell might have mentioned she was looking for someone to dig up some old photographs from a couple of decades ago. While I don't normally use the services of Frank Taranto, he is the only guy in town I could think of who might have been able to help her."

"If you think of anything else." Cutter put one of his business cards on the top of the hundred-dollar bill and slid both of them across the desk to Prentice. Faster than I would have thought possible, the cash and card disappeared into a desk drawer.

As we were leaving I asked Cutter, "Why the urgency for the DNA comparison?"

"I'd like to have the paternity issue tied up by six o'clock."

"What happens at six o'clock?" Sunny asked.

"That's about the time Nathaniel Goodman's Gulfstream will be landing at Lunken Airport."

CHAPTER NINETEEN

THE OFFICE OF A-1 Rapid Test was in a strip mall a notch above the one where Prentice's office had been located, but it would hardly qualify as plush. The waiting area was small but clean with the faint whiff of chemicals mixed with some strong disinfectants in the air. Hanging on the wall were posters of the services they offered. They ran the gamut from employer drug screening, to checking for STDs and HIV, to legally admissible paternity DNA tests. I would have been hard pressed to decide what was more depressing: the list of tests available or the fact that the ten-seat lobby was standing room only.

As we approached the check-in desk, Sunny and I made eye contact and silently agreed to let John Cutter do all the talking. Despite spending much of my youth immersed in gritty hard-boiled detective novels, I was clearly out of my element. This was John Cutter's world and not ours. Glancing again at the list of tests offered, I also made a personal commitment to not touch anything unless it was absolutely necessary, and to wash my hands as soon as possible after we left.

The sign-in desk was even more depressing. On either side of the window were large posters stating that no drugs were stored at this facility and there was twenty-four-hour surveillance. On the countertop, next to a stack of clipboards with pens attached to them by sturdy wires, was a Plexiglas document holder indicating no tests would be administered without first producing a government-approved photo ID.

Great. It takes less ID to vote than to find out whether you have gonorrhea.

On the other side of the window was a slightly plump, completely bored receptionist in her early twenties, playing a game on her phone. She had short cropped ultra-black hair, Goth make-up, and a nose stud, and was wearing a long-sleeve shirt that I suspected was mandated by management to hide her ink. Catching us in her peripheral vision, without taking her eyes off her game, she motioned with her free hand to the stack of clipboards and said, "Fill out the top page and sign the HIPAA release form. We only take cash or credit card. No personal checks."

I mentally slapped myself on the forehead. I had checked Mom's checking account but not her credit card statement. I was starting to make Janet Evanovich's Stephanie Plum look like a genius.

"I want to see Lenny," Cutter said harshly.

This caused the receptionist to at least glance up from her game. She sized Cutter up and ignored us as she reached for the phone. "Lenny, there's a cop here to see you... Okay." She turned attention back to us. "Office at the end of the hall." She buzzed us in through a heavy security door, then went back to her game.

Lenny was probably around thirty, but it had been a tough thirty. He was scrawny and a bit twitchy. The color of his badly nicotine-stained fingers matched the yellow of his teeth. "You Cutter?" he asked.

Cutter nodded.

"You paying in cash?"

Cutter nodded again.

Lenny guided us into a tiny office that was so small, the four of us barely fit. He walked around a battered desk then flopped heavily into an office chair that looked like something he had found while dumpster diving. Since it was the only chair in the office, he didn't invite us to sit down.

"Give me the father's file and two grand and I'll have results in four hours."

Cutter glanced at Sunny and me, then nodded his head toward the exit. Without a word, Cutter turned and started to leave the room.

"Hold up! Hold up!" Lenny said with a hint of panic in his voice. "I can do it for fifteen hundred."

"I can get it done for a grand in ten different places." Cutter pulled his wad of cash out of his pocket and laid nine one hundred dollar bills on the desk.

Lenny could count. "That's only nine hundred."

"Because you tried to dick me around and wasted my time, you're going to give me a ten percent discount. Non-negotiable."

When Lenny hesitated, Cutter started to reach for the cash, but Lenny's hand got there first. Cutter grabbed Lenny's wrist and squeezed. "Next time you talk to Prentice, tell him I'm not the easy mark he thinks I am. I'll pay fair market price for what I get, but I won't be gouged by a little floater like you." Cutter squeezed a bit harder, and his cold eyes locked on Lenny's. "Now you say, 'yes, sir; thank you, sir.'"

Lenny gulped and got even more twitchy. "Yes, sir. Thank you, sir."

"Good," Cutter said as he released Lenny's wrist and reached for his briefcase. He put a file folder containing a copy of the DNA data from the hair from Peterson's wig on the desktop. "Prentice said you have Elizabeth Maxwell's DNA on file." Cutter nodded in my direction. "I want a paternity comparison with her." Cutter's eyes narrowed, and his voice dropped to a level so soft it was difficult to even hear. "If I don't have my results within four hours, I'll expect a full refund." Cutter hesitated, then added, "Plus interest, if you get my meaning."

Lenny was a quick learner. He said, "Yes, sir. Thank you, sir."

The swab sample Lenny took from the inside of my cheek left an odd aftertaste in my mouth, but the taste wasn't bad enough to get me to muster up the courage to use the water fountain in the hallway as we were leaving.

Once back outside I asked Cutter, "What was the deal with Lenny?"

Cutter shrugged. "When Lenny knew my name, it meant Prentice had talked to him and marked me as a soft touch." Cutter chuckled. "As soon as Lenny has a cigarette and calms down, he'll call Prentice and tell him how I slapped him around."

"This helps us how?" Sunny asked.

"I've worked with guys like Prentice and his posse before. They're all hustlers and, for a small cut, will send business to a close circle of associates ranging from bail bondsmen to PIs like Taranto. Lenny sent your mom to Prentice; Prentice sends us to Lenny; they all scratch each other's backs. As soon as he hears from Lenny, Prentice will call Taranto and give him a heads up that I'm not the guy you want to mess with. That should make him more agreeable."

"Huh," Sunny said. "Fascinating."

"Every move is carefully planned," Cutter said, then added, "Except when it isn't."

Back at the car, John Cutter dialed the number for Frank Taranto on his cell phone and set it on the roof of the Crown Vic, then put it on speaker so we all could hear.

A sweet female voice answered. "Taranto Investigations. How may I direct your call?"

"Frank Taranto," Cutter said gruffly.

"Hold, please."

There was a brief musical interlude of a sappy instrumental version of — I thought, but wouldn't have sworn to it — a song popular from the 1960s.

"At least he's got a receptionist," Cutter said dismissively. "Considering the circles Prentice runs in, that's more than I expected."

My mind flashed to the antihero of any number of my favorite hard-boiled mysteries. I could see Taranto sitting at his battered desk with a bottle of Scotch in his lower desk drawer. A tough guy like Cutter, and immortalized by the famous Raymond Chandler quote:

Down these mean streets a man must go who is not himself mean, who is neither tarnished nor afraid. The detective in this kind of story must be such a man. He is the hero, he is everything. He must be a complete man and a common man and yet an unusual man. He must be, to use a rather weathered phrase, a man of honor, by instinct, by inevitability, without thought of it, and certainly without saying it. He must be the best man in his world and a good enough man for any world.

I had a feeling — after our sojourn this morning to the dark underbelly of a world which, because of my reading habit, I always suspected existed but had never visited — that Frank Taranto was going to be a younger version of John Cutter.

The sweet voice returned to the line. "I'm sorry, but Mr. Taranto is in a meeting with a client and has asked to not be disturbed. Would you like his voice mail?"

"Tell Mr. Taranto you have someone on the line who will pay him $1,000 for five minutes of his time if he can see us this morning."

"Excuse me?" the sweet voice said.

"You heard me, cupcake."

Cupcake?

"Also tell him I'll pay cash and won't ask for a receipt." Cutter paused. "Tell him the price I'll be willing to pay will drop to $500 if he can't fit us in until this afternoon and by this time tomorrow I won't need him at all."

"Hold, please."

More elevator music.

"Mr. Taranto will be able to see you anytime this morning," she said.

"We should be there in a few minutes. Tell him it involves the work he did for Elizabeth Maxwell."

"Your name, sir?"

"Cash. Johnny Cash." Cutter disconnected.

"Why are you willing to pay him so much?" I asked.

"Two reasons," Cutter answered. "First to show him I'm serious. And second, and most important, I think he has information we can use and I want him to share it with us."

"Why do you suspect that?"

"Thick as a brick," Sunny said with a sigh. "Mr. Cutter thinks Mom used whatever information she got from Taranto to track down Mr. MAJIC."

Cutter nodded his agreement.

"What?" I objected. "If she had found him, why not just tell me instead of putting me through all of this?"

"You know Mom," Sunny said. "She always liked to have us figure out things for ourselves. I'm just guessing here, but I think she wasn't sure how you would react to the news of your newfound Daddy Dearest. She has been sprinkling breadcrumbs for you to follow in case you wanted to figure out who he is and where to find him. But, if you weren't interested, then she has given you multiple off-ramps. Typical Mom."

Sunny was right. That was a typical Mom move.

With me temporarily thrown off stride by her comment, Sunny was able to call shotgun, which was fine with me, and I climbed into the backseat. There was something I wanted to do anyway. Before Cutter

114

had his Crown Vic in reverse, I had pulled up the pdf of Mom's and Peterson's book on my iPhone.

CHAPTER ONE

Sorting the Wheat from the Chaff

There are many paths to enlightenment and many techniques to help guide you along your way. Be open-minded and willing to try new things from yoga, to structured meditation, to diet, to controlling your breathing, to various releasing techniques, etc.

Here are the important things to remember.

- *A technique that works today may serve you well for your entire lifetime or may not work tomorrow or ever again.*
- *When a technique stops working, you should take that as a blessing. It may mean you've reached the end of what your current technique has to offer and you are ready to move forward along the path.*
- *Never be afraid to try a new technique or to retry a technique that had not worked previously. What didn't work yesterday may work today. What doesn't work today may work tomorrow.*
- *Relax your mind and listen to the silence.*
- *You are your own best spiritual guide.*
- *Be honest with yourself. On a primal level, you know what is right and what is wrong for you.*

WARNING

Like it is written in Ecclesiastes 3:1 "There is a time for everything, and a season for every activity under the heavens." Many techniques might work for a tiny fraction of people for a period of time, but the progress created by a technique may be fleeting, negligible, or even nonexistent for you. Focus on the techniques that have stood the test of time and risen to the top of major philosophies, religions, and spiritual systems. Do not allow yourself to be swept up by the hot new technique everyone is trying and talking about. Do what is right for you, not the masses.

- *If anyone tries to tell you theirs is the only true way and the reason you are blocked is you are not doing their technique properly — run from them as fast as you can. They likely are defending their technique for their own personal and/or financial reasons.*

- *Many of those who have transitioned are good people with good intentions. But it is often difficult for them to communicate in helpful ways with those still on the path. There's a tendency on the other side to believe that you know "what's best" for others. The exact opposite is almost always true. Those who have transitioned have forgotten what it is like to be you and usually cannot provide advice that is helpful. Hardly surprising, they will only recommend the techniques that worked for them and not necessarily be positive about different techniques that might help you.*

- *Beyond that, the self-help arena is heavily populated with wishful thinkers who cannot help themselves but think they can help you, and even charlatans and con men who, in addition to NOT helping you find your way, may actually be a barrier to overcome in your enlightenment quest.*

I should know. I was one of those people.

I felt the car slowing, and I glanced up to see us pulling into the parking lot of a small office building.

CHAPTER TWENTY

FTER OUR VISITS to the offices of Wilson Prentice, attorney-at-law, and A-1 Rapid Tests, the office of Taranto Investigations was not at all what I expected. The office index in the lobby of the sleek three-story building listed a variety of accountants, architects, a real estate title company, and several law offices. Even more surprising was the fact Taranto's office had the entire top floor.

When we stepped off the elevator, we were immediately able to put a name and a face to the sweet voice we had heard earlier. The nameplate sitting in front of the fair-skinned blonde with azure eyes and startlingly white teeth read *Cheryl Winters*. Behind her we could see twenty oversized workstations, each equipped with multiple computer monitors and mostly manned by males young enough to be Sunny's and my kid brother.

"Ah, Mr. John Cutter, Ms. Grace Maxwell, and Ms. Sunny Maxwell," Cheryl said with a radiant smile. "Mr. Taranto is expecting you." Cheryl pointed a manicured finger toward the left side corridor.

"Which door?" Cutter asked.

"There is only one."

"How did she know our names?" I asked as we headed down the corridor.

Cutter looked at me in disbelief and sighed.

Sunny answered for him. "Since Mom obviously has one of her plans in motion here, Taranto probably was expecting us the same way Prentice was."

"Oh, yeah, that makes sense. But how did he know Cutter's name? He told him he was Johnny Cash," I protested.

Cutter snorted. "Ever heard of caller ID?"

"Or Prentice could have told him," Sunny added.

Before I could embarrass myself any further, a petite young man, probably just north of thirty, dressed in skinny-legged blue jeans and a black golf shirt with *Taranto Investigations* embroidered above the left breast, stepped out of the office we were approaching. To get to five feet six inches and a hundred and fifty pounds, he would have needed lifts in his shoes and diving weights in his pockets. We all assumed he was Frank Taranto's assistant, but we were in for a shock.

The young man extended his hand to Cutter. "Frank Taranto. Come in, come in."

If this was the prototype of the modern detective, somewhere Dashiell Hammett and Raymond Chandler were spinning in their graves.

Once inside his office, it was clear why Taranto Investigations needed the entire top floor. Frank Taranto's private office was huge. I mean, big enough to have half a dozen '70s-era video games, three pinball machines, a foosball table, and a pool table. Mounted on the walls were twelve sixty-inch flat-screen TVs all silently playing news and financial channels. Hidden speakers where softly playing classic rock.

I started to say something, but I was at a loss for words, so I just shook my head.

Frank Taranto motioned us in the direction of four comfortable overstuffed chairs arranged in a square where we could chat and see each other.

Taranto turned to Sunny and me. "I only met your mom twice, but I really liked her. My condolences on your loss."

"You seem to be remarkably well informed," Cutter said gruffly.

"You gave me fifteen minutes to do a background check before your arrival," Taranto said as he turned to Sunny. "We have a mutual acquaintance, William Hanson."

"You know who I'm dating?" Sunny said in disbelief.

Taranto just smiled. "Welcome to the Brave New World. There is precious little my guys can't find if it has got even a whiff of an electronic footprint. For example..." Taranto turned to Cutter. "John Adams Cutter of Hendersonville, N.C. Twenty-eight years with the

NYPD. Retired under duress as a senior homicide detective following the S.A. Peterson case." Taranto turned to me. "Grace Bliss Maxwell. Perfect score on your SAT in high school with a full ride to Columbia University. Graduated top of your class in English lit…"

"Okay," Cutter said gruffly as he fished his iPad mini out of his jacket pocket. "You made your point." Cutter hit a few keys on his tablet and began reading out loud from the screen. "Francis Sheldon Taranto. Terminated six years ago from the Cincinnati Police Department forensics science division for gross insubordination."

Taranto nodded his approval. "I think I may have underestimated you, Mr. Cutter. Old school and you've got computer chops. Nice combination. Those records were sealed when I agreed to resign; I'm surprised you were able to access them, especially that quickly," Taranto said as he continued to size up Cutter. "For the record, my boss was an idiot, and his boss had to have his assistant print out his emails because he couldn't figure out how to read them otherwise. May I ask who provides you with your tech support?"

"Yes."

"Yes what?" Taranto asked.

"Yes, you may ask."

Taranto laughed. "Okay. Who provides you with your technical support?"

"Nathaniel Goodman," Cutter answered.

"Whoa! Seriously?" Taranto leaned back in his chair. "How could my guys have missed something like that when they did your background check?"

"Maybe your guys aren't as good as you think. Being hooked up with a clown show like Wilson Prentice certainly doesn't enhance your mystique," Cutter stated flatly.

"I had never dealt with Prentice before Elizabeth Maxwell walked through the door. We're a bit pricey for his usual clientele. But, we don't turn away legal and above-board business, even from a bottom feeder like Prentice."

I saw that as an opening to get back on message. "What did my mother want?" I asked.

"She wanted a copy of every photograph of S.A. Peterson we could find."

"That sounds like pretty routine stuff that you would turn over to one of your research people," Cutter said. "How did it move up the food chain to your desk?"

"Half of my guys, me included, would give up their first born for a chance to work for William Hanson. When one of them did the preliminary, pre-appointment background check, he discovered the Maxwell sister had gone to high school with Hanson. He brought it to me and I reached out to him." Taranto gave Sunny a smile. "William Hanson asked me to take a personal interest."

"Why?" Sunny demanded.

"And you say I'm dense," I said with a snort. "That was what, four months ago? Willie was hoping to use it to help him get you in bed."

Taranto touched the end of his nose with his index finger, then pointed to me. "Having now met you," Taranto said to Sunny, "I can see what all of the fuss was about."

"What did you find?" Cutter asked as he tried to steer the conversation back on topic.

"While Peterson was a public figure, there were remarkably few photographs to start with. Plus, he disappeared long before publications had an online presence, so even the pictures we could find were low-quality newspaper halftones. It took some digging, but we eventually were able to track down some original prints we could convert into hi-res jpegs. We started out with the usual stuff that had appeared in local and national newspapers that had been archived on their websites. A couple of publications did features on the tenth anniversary of his disappearance — those appeared in their online editions, which helped. We hit the mother lode when we stumbled across a Peterson tribute page on Facebook. Apparently, some guy who worked for him had taken a butt load of black and white pictures with his tiny Leica 35mm camera that were in clear violation of his nondisclosure agreement. We convinced him enough time had passed for him to safely put them online, where we immediately snatched them up. A few days later, he pulled the Facebook page down. When I talked to him, he said he had gotten a nasty phone call from a lawyer that put the fear of God in him." Taranto chuckled. "It didn't matter to us; we had copies of his entire portfolio."

"What did you do next?" Cutter asked.

"We gave the entire bundle to Elizabeth Maxwell. A couple of days later, she called me and thanked me for our help, but said she would not be needing our services any longer."

"Why not?" I demanded.

Taranto shrugged. "She said she had just found Simon Peterson."

CHAPTER TWENTY-ONE

"YES! Way to go Mom!" Sunny said excitedly and extended a fist bump in my direction.

I was too stunned to react. I glanced in the direction of John Cutter, and he was gray in the face and even more flabbergasted than me.

Cutter, having regained a measure of composure, cleared his throat. "How much help did you give Mrs. Maxwell in locating Peterson?"

"None. All we provided to her was a packet of old photographs. Apparently, she did the rest."

Cutter leaned in on his elbows and glared threateningly at Taranto. "I have trouble believing that a housewife with late-stage cancer could have found somebody through a few old snapshots in a couple of days that I've been trying to track down for two decades without some serious outside help."

"I love the way you lean in and look all hostile. Does that tough guy thing ever work?" Taranto asked with a laugh. Cutter's hostile expression didn't change, and Taranto dismissed it with a wave of his hand. "All we did was provide a block of photographs."

"Can we get copies of the pictures you gave my mom?" Sunny asked.

"I'll need the approval of the executor of her estate," Taranto answered.

"No problem," Sunny answered. "I'm the executor."

"You are?" I asked incredulously.

"Why?" Sunny asked with a laugh. "Do you want to file a legal challenge to me handling the estate?"

"No," I answered. "I just want to know how it happened."

"Process of elimination, big sis. You were the absentee daughter, I'm in town and prelaw, and, most importantly, do you really want Dad trying to handle legal documents?"

"All good points," I said as Sunny pulled out her phone and opened a pdf and turned it around to show Taranto.

"Here's our mom's will."

Taranto nodded his approval and handed Sunny his business card. "Send it to me."

"Email or text?"

"Email," Taranto said, "then it will be archived on our servers."

Instead of typing in the email address herself, Sunny handed Taranto her phone. His fingers danced on her screen and a moment later, his phone chirped. "Got it," he said as he gave Sunny her phone back. He reached into his front shirt pocket and handed Sunny a thumb drive.

Sunny laughed. "You were expecting us to ask for this, and you were ready."

Taranto shrugged and smiled. "Your mother authorized me to release the pictures but only to the executor of her estate."

"Oh, Mom!" Sunny said.

John Cutter chuckled. "Nice," he muttered to no one in particular.

Despite multiple cups of Dad's coffee and several thousand mystery novels under my belt, I wasn't sharp enough to catch the significance of Mom's instructions. Sunny saw the puzzled look on my face.

"Mom, obviously, knew I was the executor of her estate."

I motioned for my sister to continue. "And."

"Without me, you don't get the file." Tears welled up in Sunny's eyes. "The way she has set this up, Mom either wanted us to look for Peterson together or not at all."

I'll be damned. Sunny is right.

Then it hit me.

"I've seen that look before," Sunny said as she saw the expression on my face. "What gives?"

"I think we can agree that Mom planned this entire snipe hunt from the beginning."

Sunny nodded.

"Mom has given us a series of problems with opportunities for me to bail at any time."

"Obviously," Sunny answered.

I pointed at the USB drive in Sunny's hand. "The bad news; I'll give long odds that drive is just another piece of the puzzle."

"What's the good news?" Sunny asked.

"The solution will be cracking the password to her cloud account."

"How is that good news?" Sunny asked.

"She wants us to work for it, but she also wants us to find it."

"Oh man!" Sunny exclaimed. "It is hidden in plain sight!"

"Bingo!"

"That changes everything. We need to start thinking like Mom."

"That will be easier for you than for me," I said with a grunt.

"You're right, and that changes everything again."

"Why?"

"She would want you to find it, not me," Sunny said as her eyes unfocused and her mind began working in overdrive. "We need to be thinking like you and not Mom." Sunny closed her eyes and rubbed her forehead. "Trying to think like you is already starting to give me a headache."

I slugged her in the shoulder.

John Cutter cleared his throat, which brought Sunny and me back to reality. "Or maybe we'll see what she saw in the pictures and figure it out without having to access her cloud account."

"My guys are pretty good hackers," Taranto offered. "Maybe I could help."

"Right," Sunny said with a laugh. "Are they good enough to hack one of William's servers?"

"Does the password use William's four-word, three-special-character rule?"

"If we had the password, we would know the answer to that question, now, wouldn't we?" Sunny answered playfully. "William doesn't know for sure, but he thinks so."

"Let me think. Can we hack a file William Hanson can't get into on a server he has in his physical possession? Hmm," Taranto said as he scratched his chin and stared off into space for a moment. "The answer is no. I take that back. The answer is hell no. My guys are good, but nobody is good enough to hack something Hanson can't."

I was getting more and more impressed with Sunny's boyfriend.

"How many pictures are on the drive?" Cutter asked.

"Seven hundred and forty-two," Taranto answered. "Mostly they're pretty crappy, often backstage and low-light crowd shots. I've reviewed the pictures, and I have no idea what Elizabeth Maxwell saw that I didn't." Taranto's eyes locked on Cutter. "You probably need to consider that the timing of her receiving the pictures and allegedly finding S. A. Peterson could be coincidental and not related."

I drew in a breath through my nose, then slowly released it. "He has a point," I said. "Which brings us back to the cloud drive we can't access."

Cutter glared at Taranto. "I'm going to ask you point-blank, Taranto, and if you lie to me, you will personally regret it. Do you know the whereabouts of the man claiming to be Simon Alphonse Peterson?"

"I love the tough guy persona!" Taranto chuckled. "No. I do not know who this man is or where to find him." Taranto grinned like the cat that had caught the canary. "You, of course, know," Taranto said smugly, "that Peterson is a stolen identity."

Taranto's expected bombshell fizzled. Badly.

"Of course I know that," Cutter answered.

"Oh really?" Taranto said, sounding unconvinced.

"He died when he was a few days old in Little Rock, Arkansas."

"He showed me a copy of the death certificate," I added.

Taranto leaned back in his chair again and looked at Cutter with new eyes. "Well, I'll be damned," Taranto said, "now I'm really impressed. If you're ever looking for work, let me know."

"With all of your technology, why would you want an old war horse like me?" Cutter asked.

"I can find people," Taranto answered with a laugh. "But I still need someone to bring them in. How long have you known Peterson was a fake ID?"

"Over twenty years."

"Wow. This Peterson guy had built one of the best fake identities we've ever seen, and nine hundred ninety-nine out of a thousand investigators would have certified him as the real deal. For you to have figured out he was dead before the Little Rock public records went online — and to have kept it to yourself all of these years — is damned amazing." Taranto shook his head. "With that level of attention to detail, I can see why you're pissed Elizabeth Maxwell found Peterson before you."

Cutter's face darkened. Taranto had hit a nerve. "We only have your word that she told you she had found Peterson."

Taranto smiled and picked up a remote control that was laying on the coffee table in front of him. "I thought you might say that." He pushed a button and the background music stopped and the room filled with a voice from the grave.

"Mr. Taranto, this is Elizabeth Maxwell. I wanted to thank you for all of your help and to let you know because of the pictures you located I've been able to find Simon Peterson. Mr. Prentice said he would handle the billing so if you will send him your invoice I'll pay it immediately. Again, thanks for all of your help."

Sunny and I gaped at each other with our mouths open. Cutter shook his head in disbelief.

"We archive all voice mails and phone conversations," Taranto said matter-of-factly.

Before any of us could regain our footing, Cutter's phone beeped. He glanced at the screen, then turned to me.

"Speaking of proof. Your probability of paternity from the DNA samples we have of Peterson and your birth mother are over 99.99 percent. The man who was claimed to be Simon Alphonse Peterson is definitely your biological father."

Surprised by our tepid reaction to the news, Taranto asked, "I assume that's good, right?"

Cutter shrugged. "It just confirms what we had already suspected, but it doesn't get us any closer to actually finding Peterson."

CHAPTER TWENTY-TWO

I LET SUNNY HAVE the front seat again. The mood in the car was somber as we headed back to our house. We all now knew the man claiming to be Peterson was indeed my father, which, for me at least, was more unnerving than reassuring and generated more questions than answers. Who was this man? What motivated him? Why did he create the fake persona? Why did he vanish? Had Mom really never told him about me? Is that why he never tried to find me?

I felt a headache building.

I used Sunny's breathing technique, which helped a little, but not nearly enough. With a sigh, I reopened the pdf of my mother's and — I couldn't believe I was thinking this — my father's book.

CHAPTER TWO

If it is so simple, why isn't everyone enlightened?

The True Path of Enlightenment can be easy and smooth, or bumpy. It's mostly your choice.

There are no "silver bullets" or "magic pills." There is no one-size-fits-all technique. You must find the techniques that work for you. When you do, MAJIC happens – rapidly.

Most people don't attain enlightenment during meditation or other spiritual techniques. In fact, having what you believe is a great meditation session may mean very little. It might even set you back by pointing you in the wrong direction.

To determine whether a technique is working for you, ask this question. After using a specific technique, did it change your daily life for the better?

Often the hardest concept for people on the path to grasp is the limitation of our symbolic thought. Our minds turn everything into symbols that can be analyzed and mulled over ad nauseam.

Enlightened people are masters of their mind, not mastered by their mind. They live in an ongoing and persistently non-symbolic experience — free of the tyranny of symbolic thought.

To reach this place, long-held beliefs will often need to be challenged and their place in your life justified. You will have to be honest with yourself to find yourself.

Avoiding internal friction and external stress by trying to minimize them through meditation and other relaxation techniques are often counterproductive. Any peace you attain will be both transitory and short-lived.

The methods that work for you will work on the mind from outside it, not from within it.

The transition to enlightenment is just the beginning. It's akin to the concept of being "born again." After it comes learning to "live again."

As I read the words on the page, I heard my mother's voice. My entire life, she had told me about all of the exercises listed and had encouraged me to at least try them. Instead of listening, I had dug my heels in and rejected all of this out of hand. No matter how belligerent or negative my response was to her gentle suggestions, she would simply smile and say someday I would be ready, and leave me to pout in my room.

I'd always thought she was a starry-eyed fool. Now, after reading this and feeling the positive effect of the stuff Sunny had taught me, I wasn't so sure anymore.

The Crown Vic rolled to a stop at the curb in front of our house, and Cutter popped the trunk. As I pulled myself out of the backseat, Cutter grabbed his MacBook, which was in a cushioned black carrying case, and we all headed toward the door.

CHAPTER TWENTY-THREE

D AD OFFERED US food and drink, but we were only interested in seeing the photos on the thumb drive we had gotten from Frank Taranto. Cutter downloaded the folder to his MacBook first, followed by Sunny, then finally me.

When I opened the file, I was disappointed. As Taranto had warned, most of the pictures were low quality and blurry, and all were black and white. I scanned through all seven hundred and forty-two images quickly to see whether anything jumped out, but nothing did. Then I went back and gave each one a bit more time. All of the pictures by the guy Taranto had found on Facebook looked like they were taken quickly and without concern for either focus or cropping. If they hadn't had at least a glimpse of the camera-shy Peterson in each frame, more often than not in profile so he didn't see he was being photographed, they likely would have been tossed years ago.

There were a handful of photos centered around a man in his late twenties or early thirties that stood out. They were the only pictures in the entire batch without Peterson in the frame. Sunny noticed him as well.

"Any idea who this is?" Sunny asked.

"It looks like a young Nathaniel Goodman," I answered.

Cutter glanced at one of the pictures and immediately confirmed it. "Yeah, that's Goodman. Hardly surprising he would be in a few pictures since, as far as I could tell, he attended every event Peterson held."

After Cutter had done another quick review of the pictures, he stepped out of Mom's office to place a couple of calls. I assumed they were to Mark Franklin and possibly Nathaniel Goodman. I didn't know whether Cutter was trying to be polite and not disturb Sunny and me, or whether he had things he wanted to say that weren't for our ears. With Cutter, it could go either way. After about five minutes, he returned to his spot and started in on the pictures in earnest.

An hour later, I was so engrossed in the pictures, I hadn't even noticed the glass of iced tea and tuna sandwich that had magically appeared at my elbow until Sunny pointed to them. I suddenly realized, having skipped breakfast, that I was famished. I took a bite of the sandwich and smiled; it was exactly the way Dad knew I liked it. Light on the mayo and heavy on the chopped celery with a generous slice of heirloom tomato from Mom's garden on lightly toasted sourdough bakery bread.

"Dad still spoils you," Sunny said as she took a bite of her sandwich.

It took a few seconds for me to catch up; then I noticed Dad had cut the crusts off my sandwich, but not hers. In addition, he had placed one of Mom's straws next to my tea.

I didn't know whether it was fatigue, hunger, or the emotional roller coaster ride I had been on for the past two days, but that gentle act of kindness by my dad — cutting the crust off of a tuna sandwich and giving me a silly straw — brought tears to my eyes.

Sunny, seeing my reaction, moved her plate and pulled her chair so close to mine that our knees were touching. She took a bite of her sandwich, then leaned her head on my shoulder. "Dad never cuts off my crusts," she muttered softly.

I patted the top of her head. "Of course not," I said whimsically. "We both know he always liked me best."

"Or, he knew if he didn't cut them off, you'd storm off to your room all pouty, and we wouldn't see you again for a couple of days." Sunny gave me a nudge. "Sometimes I think he forgot on purpose just so we didn't have to be around you when you were in one of your moods."

We both giggled.

It was easily the best sandwich I had ever eaten in my entire life.

After we were finished, Sunny and I carried the dishes back to the kitchen, rinsed them, then put them in the dishwasher. When we got back to Mom's office, John Cutter was leaning back in his chair with his fingers interlocked behind his head, glaring at his computer and yawning. "If your mother saw something in these pictures, then I certainly don't see it."

"Do you think Taranto might have been right and Mom found a

clue somewhere else and these pictures are worthless?" Sunny asked.

Cutter rolled his neck and yawned again. "I hope not. For the moment, since we can't figure out the password, this is our only active lead."

I was tired, but John Cutter was exhausted. Here was a guy in his seventies who had been functioning at his peak on only a couple of hours of sleep after driving three hundred miles in the middle of the night to get here. Until now, he had been able to get by on the adrenaline rush of the possibility that he might be solving the case that had ended his career and haunted him for twenty-four years. Now that the investigation had hit a wall, the energy and enthusiasm seemed to have leaked out of him, and he was showing his age.

Sunny noticed it too and shouted, "Dad!"

Dad stuck his head in the office with an annoyed expression on his face. He always hated shouting in the house. "What?"

"Mr. Cutter needs a shower and a nap..."

"That's really not necessary," Cutter protested.

"You've got time for a two-hour nap before we have to pick up Mr. Goodman at the airport." Sunny folded her arms and glared at Cutter. "Go."

Before Cutter could protest, I said, "Don't waste your time trying to argue with her. You know she's right, and we've got you outnumbered."

Cutter's eyes moved from Sunny to me to Dad, and since he could count, he ran up the white flag without further protests. "I appreciate it," he muttered as he pulled himself heavily to his feet.

"You can use the shower in the master bedroom and catch a few winks in there without worrying about walking in on one of the girls," Dad said. "I'll get you some fresh towels."

Since we were getting nowhere with the photographs, Sunny and I decided to take a break as well.

I wandered back upstairs to the cave and tried to reengage with my novel, but my mind kept drifting back to what Sunny had said.

What the heck.

I put the paperback on my nightstand next to my golden straw, stretched out flat on my back and closed my eyes. I started with Sunny's easy breathing exercise. I did that for about two minutes until I started feeling light-headed.

In for penny; in for a pound.

I moved on to Sunny's next breathing exercise. At first it was hard to concentrate on breathing through my heart since every few seconds, random thoughts from my head tried to intrude. Finally, I was able to focus on my dad and the incredible amount of affection he had shown me my entire life. I was able to stay with that feeling for a long while, as the flood of good memories of his unconditional love lifted my spirits and my heart sent the love back to him.

As Dad began to drift away, he was replaced by Sunny. I knew she and I had now fully and totally connected. We were now more than just sisters, we were friends. My heart soared as I knew we would be sharing a lifetime of adventures that would dwarf those in any of the novels I had ever read.

Then, suddenly, my focus shifted to my mom.

Love can be bittersweet.

She knew I loved her, and she loved me. But with so much history between us, I felt blocked and had trouble making the same connection I had with my dad and Sunny. Forcing myself to relax and chasing away intruding noise from my head, I focused on my heart and my mom. Finally, I felt my thoughts go silent, and all I heard was the beating of my heart, and all I could feel was my mother's love. I was a little girl again, safe in her arms.

Mommy.

***

When Sunny tapped on the door, I glanced at the clock on my nightstand and was stunned to discover I had been asleep for almost two hours. I didn't ever remember sleeping so deeply in my life. Time had stood completely still, and I had fallen into a well of mental silence.

I tried to speak and failed badly. I cleared my throat and tried again. My voice was still froggy, but at least I was audible. "Come in."

Sunny popped her head in. "We're leaving to pick up Goodman at the airport in about thirty minutes and..." Sunny stopped midsentence and gave me an odd stare. "Well, look at you!"

"What?" I demanded.

"You've been doing the technique I suggested."

"Maybe," I answered as I tossed off the sheet, pulled myself into a sitting position, and pivoted my feet to the floor. "How can you tell?"

"I can read you like one of your silly books," Sunny answered with a snort.

"Right."

"Can you tell if a person is happy or sad or angry?" Sunny asked.

"Sure, it's called body language," I answered with a grunt. "Is there a point here somewhere?"

"There is," Sunny answered brightly. "Your conscious mind hates things it can't explain logically. Maybe when you think you're reading body language, you're actually reading, for want of a better name, a person's aura on a subconscious level. Maybe your conscious mind is translating what it's seeing into something that won't scare the crap out of you and give you nightmares."

I closed my eyes and rubbed my forehead. "Really? Auras?" I asked.

"Remember what Mom used to call me when we were kids?"

"Sure, her little silver streak. But I always thought that was because you liked to run around naked in the backyard until you were six."

"Nope," Sunny said with a laugh. "According to Mom, silver has been my default aura color for my entire life."

"You buy this whole aura reading thing?"

"Me? Not for one second," Sunny answered with a laugh.

"But Mom did?" I asked.

"Oh yeah. Big time."

"Wow!" I put both of my hands on my cheeks in amazement. "You mean there are actually a few things Mom said that you didn't swallow hook, line, and sinker?"

"Mom and I argued about stuff all the time," Sunny replied defensively.

"Really?" I said in disbelief. "Like what?"

"We can talk about that later, but now you need to get it in gear."

"Why?"

"I'm pretty sure John Cutter is not going to be late picking up his boss because you haven't finished powdering your nose."

CHAPTER TWENTY-FOUR

SUNNY HAD BEEN absolutely right about Cutter; he had the driver's side door open and was checking his watch and tapping his fingers on the roof of the Crown Vic as I sprinted out the door and down the steps. I suspected I was about thirty seconds away from seeing whether my Uber app worked as well in suburban Cincinnati as it did in NYC.

"Sorry," I muttered as I dove into the backseat.

Cutter glared at me as he climbed in behind the wheel. His little repose had worked miracles. Once again he looked like if you messed with him in public, the YouTube video of you getting your ass kicked by a man who had been collecting Social Security checks for half a decade would have over a million hits. All of my hard-boiled authors would have loved this guy.

Living on the east side of Cincinnati, we were not fighting the outbound rush-hour traffic when we headed west to get to Lunken Airport. Known as "Sunken Lunken" by the locals, the executive airport was set in a low spot with dikes on three sides and a hill on the other to keep the waters of the Little Miami and Ohio Rivers at bay during flood season. Only a few miles from downtown and with a long runway, it was home to many of the private and corporate jets in the Tristate area. It was big enough that it had daily shuttle services to five different cities, allowing business people to avoid the hassle of dealing with Cincinnati/Northern Kentucky International Airport.

Once again, alone in the backseat and with time to kill, I pulled up the pdf of Mom's book and started reading a section how family relationships can be challenging.

Sunny, unable to generate much conversation with John Cutter, looked over the seat in my direction. "Whatcha doin'?" she asked brightly.

I turned my phone around so she could see what I was reading.

"Ah," she answered. "I read Mom's book while you were snoozing. It's really good."

"Wait? What?" I said in disbelief. "You read the whole thing while I was napping?"

"Unlike some people, who shall remain nameless, I don't slave over every word I read like it is etched on a stone tablet fresh from the summit of Mount Sinai." Sunny laughed, then continued, "Besides, none of this is new to me. Her book is basically a manifesto of the way she lived her life and the way I pray I continue to live mine."

Cutter's iPhone, which was in one of the cup holders in the console separating the two front seats, chirped, "In one quarter mile, make a right-hand turn onto Wilmer Avenue. Then go five hundred feet and make a right turn onto Airport Road."

Two minutes later, we were approaching a security hut where an overweight kid in a rent-a-cop uniform that was half a size too small was waiting. The gatekeeper glanced at his clipboard as we rolled to a stop. Even before the driver's side window was all the way down, the kid had started to wave us through. "Please take the first hard left, Mr. Cutter," the guard said with as much of a professional tone as he was capable of mustering. "You'll see the other cars."

If John Cutter was surprised by any of this, he didn't show it. I hadn't really thought it through, but in retrospect, I guessed it might have been too much to expect a guy with ten zeros in his net worth to squeeze into the backseat of Cutter's car next to me.

Turning the corner, we saw a black Range Rover and a stretch limo parked on the tarmac. Two men in dark suits, who looked like they could have served with William's bodyguard in some dusty and hot foreign war, were leaning against the side of the limo. Seeing another car approaching, they immediately spread out. One went to the far side of the limo, and the other began walking in our direction while holding up his left hand, requesting us to stop. I wouldn't have sworn to it, but I thought they each had a pistol in their hand.

Cutter rolled to a stop twenty yards short of the pair. "You two stay put until I tell you." Before getting out, Cutter looked directly at

Sunny. "This is not the time to do anything you might think is cute or clever. These are not the kind of men who take kindly to unexpected movement or surprises."

"What are you looking at me for?" Sunny objected.

"If she reaches for the door handle, I'll tackle her," I offered.

Cutter nodded, then slowly opened the driver's side door, and made an obvious show that both of his hands were empty and well away from his body. "Cutter, John Cutter," he shouted in the direction of the two bodyguards. The man behind the limo stayed put, and the other man, who I could now see did have a weapon in his right hand, approached Cutter.

"ID," he shouted. I'm not an expert on guns, but it looked to me like the guy in the suit closest to us used his thumb to release the safety on the automatic he held loosely at his right side.

Sunny and I were transfixed as we watched all this play out.

Cutter slowly opened his jacket front with his left hand so they both could see the absence of any weapon on his belt, then, just using his thumb and index finger, pulled out his wallet. The first man stopped about ten feet from Cutter and motioned for him to toss him the wallet. Cutter did it like he had done it a thousand times before. The first man caught it without ever taking his eyes off of Cutter. He thumbed through the wallet, then nodded to his partner, and both of them holstered their weapons.

"Are those the Maxwell sisters in the car?" the first man asked as he returned Cutter's wallet.

"Yes," Cutter answered.

"Please wait in your vehicle until Mr. Goodman's plane has landed and the stairs have been extended."

"Of course." Cutter tucked his wallet back where it belonged and then got back in the car.

"That was intense," Sunny said as she patted her chest.

"Not really," Cutter relied. "Just routine, good bodyguard work. It's always a pleasure to deal with pros." Cutter pointed in the distance to a sleek sixteen-passenger jet that was roaring down the runway in our direction.

"Nice," Sunny said "That's a Gulfstream G650."

"How would you possibly know that?" I asked.

"William is thinking about buying one, but apparently there is like a two-year waiting list for a new one."

"How much do one of those things cost?"

Sunny just shrugged. "Not a clue."

I Googled *G650 price*, and my eyes nearly popped out of my head when I saw the jet's price started at $65 million and only went up from there.

"How much money does William have?" I demanded.

Sunny shrugged. "I've never asked. A lot, I guess."

The Gulfstream rolled to a stop a few hundred feet from the limo and the Range Rover, and as the engines began to quiet down, the side door opened and flipped down to make a set of stairs. In the doorway, another man in a dark suit eyed the tarmac and got a thumbs up from the two drivers before coming down the steps. The man who had checked Cutter's ID motioned for us to approach.

Cutter reached for the door latch. "Watch your manners, ladies. It's showtime."

CHAPTER TWENTY-FIVE

WE ARRIVED AT the bottom of the Gulfstream's staircase at the exact same moment Nathaniel Goodman arrived at the door at the top of the steps. When he saw us, like every other man with a pulse and a still functioning penis, his eyes locked on Sunny. He had an odd expression on his face and nearly dropped the cellphone he had been talking into. He immediately handed the phone to his female personal assistant, who was only half a step behind him.

"No calls," Goodman said as he descended the stairs.

Goodman was in his mid-fifties, dark complexioned, medium height, and exceedingly fit. He extended his hand to Cutter. "Excellent work, John. First rate." He turned his attention to Sunny and me but did not offer his hand. "You're Grace Maxwell," Goodman stated, and I nodded. "I assume this is your sister, Sunny."

"Yes, sir," I answered.

"I would like to see the manuscript," Goodman said bluntly.

"We left it at a secure location at the Maxwell house, sir," Cutter said.

Goodman turned and headed toward the limo. "Grace, you'll ride with me. I'm sure you have as many questions for me as I have for you." Goodman spoke with the confident tone and body language of a man who was used to getting his requests fulfilled instantly, without any questions, and never having to repeat himself. I guessed having a net worth greater than the annual gross domestic product of the bottom quarter of the countries in the United Nations would put a bit of a swagger in your step.

Sunny didn't say anything but gave me her big-eyes look.

"I would like to have my sister ride along with us," I said.

"Of course," Goodman answered without looking back as one of his bodyguards opened the rear door of the limo and the three of us piled in. The man who had checked Cutter's ID was now behind the steering wheel, and one of the men from the jet joined him in the front seat. The driver was looking in the rearview mirror, awaiting instructions. "Take us to the Maxwell house." The driver nodded and apparently didn't need directions. Pros. "Window up, please." The driver nodded again, and the glass in the partition between the front and rear sections hummed to life and began to rise.

"I normally prefer using proper names," Goodman said, "but since both of you would be Ms. Maxwell, it might be less confusing if I call you Grace and Sunny. If that is all right with both of you?"

"We prefer that, actually, Mr. Goodman," Sunny answered. She made eye contact with me and smiled when Mr. Goodman did not offer to have us call him Nat.

"I find it..."

"Excuse me, Mr. Goodman," Sunny said. "But you have been getting detailed reports from Mr. Cutter, and you already pretty much know all that we know. It might be a better usage of our time if you let my sister ask her questions first."

A flicker of a smile flashed across Goodman's face. "You are certainly your mother's daughter," Goodman answered. "Not only do you look very much like her, you sound like her as well."

Sunny nodded. "Thank you. I strive every day to be as much like her as I possibly can."

"You knew our mother?" I asked.

"Yes," Goodman answered. "We only met in person a few times, but she made quite an impression on both Simon and me."

"How well did you know Mr. Peterson?" I asked.

"We're probably as close as two people can be."

"Partners in crime?" Sunny asked.

"What crime are you referring to, Sunny?"

"As you know, we have the original report from the private investigator outlining, in excruciating details, the debauchery of members of Peterson's staff and crew."

"You've read the report?" Goodman asked.

"Yes," Sunny answered confidently. "As I'm sure Mr. Cutter informed you, the original certified copy was among our mother's things."

"Did you recall seeing either me or Simon Peterson mentioned as an active participant in any of these reprehensible activities?"

That slowed down the Sunny Express.

Goodman answered for her. "I'll take that as a no. Did it ever occur to you to ask who requested and paid for such an obviously expensive and detailed investigation and why they might have done so?"

"Son-of-a-bitch," I said as I closed my eyes and shook my head. "Of course."

"Ahh," Goodman said. "Mark Franklin told me you were bright."

Sunny slapped her forehead. "Neither you nor Peterson were involved in any of the nefarious activities, and as soon as you heard the rumors about what was going on, you hired a private investigator to get to the bottom of it."

I looked at Goodman and shook my head. "I'm just speculating here, but hopefully my father was just as offended as I was by what he read."

"Full marks, Grace." Goodman nodded his approval. "I can assure you your father was horrified. The manuscript your mother essentially wrote, with precious little input from Simon, changed his life and mine as well. We were experiencing a new reality. Our early work helped many, but it also stunted the spiritual growth of millions and millions of people. While all of this was happening, people we thought we could trust were preying on the vulnerable and damaged who were coming to us seeking fulfillment. We were trapped in a nightmare of our own making. We were already in the process of winding down the operations of the dog-and-pony-show side of the business and planned to stick exclusively to books and no longer make public appearances requiring a large staff."

"If that was the plan," I asked, "why didn't Peterson just track Mom down and explain everything?"

"Isn't it obvious?" Goodman asked.

"Maybe to you," I answered.

Sunny shook her head. "After that night in the hotel room, she felt completely betrayed and never would have believed another word Peterson would have said to her."

"Exactly," Goodman said, "and it crushed him."

"Did he know about me?"

"Absolutely not," Goodman answered. "If he had, I'm certain he would have handled things very differently, and I sincerely doubt he would have vanished."

Sunny snorted.

"What?" Goodman demanded.

"From where I sit," Sunny said, "it looks to me, with the fake identity and all of the other red flags waving around this guy, he played you for a complete fool."

"Ms. Maxwell. Sunny. Simon Peterson did not play me for a fool. I knew exactly what he was doing. In fact, I helped him do it."

CHAPTER TWENTY-SIX

I WAS AMAZED. "YOU admit to being a part of the conspiracy?"

"Again, what conspiracy?" Goodman objected. "I freely admit I helped the person known as Simon Peterson to liquidate his financial empire and to move the cash to a safe haven offshore. I will also stipulate that because of the book your mother had written and the way it impacted the man known as Simon Peterson, he became horrified by the monster he had created and had already decided to slay it. A conspiracy requires a crime, and none existed."

"Do you know where we can find Simon Peterson?" Sunny asked.

"Yes," Goodman answered.

"Where is he?" Sunny demanded.

"He's buried in Little Rock, Arkansas."

"Too clever by half," Sunny said in the same tone she had used previously on Mark Franklin. "Let me rephrase. Do you know where the man who called himself Simon Peterson is right now?"

"Let's not dance around, Sunny," Goodman said forcefully. "I am willing to swear under oath that I have not seen or spoken to the man known as Simon Alphonse Peterson in any manner or form for the past twenty-four years."

"I've noticed you tend to speak in a very precise and almost lawyerly manner," Sunny said.

"It is a habit I've gotten into. In my world, words not only have meaning, they also have a monetary value and risk potential."

"Risk potential?" I asked

"An imprecise comment, construed the wrong way, that finds itself in the media can raise or drop the value of the shares in my companies. They can also trigger a Securities and Exchange inquiry. People with deep pockets make for large targets."

"Speaking of pockets, how much of Peterson's money ended up in yours?" Sunny asked.

"None of it," Goodman answered. "And I do not appreciate the implication or your tone."

"You're a big boy, and I'm sure you've heard worse," Sunny said firmly. "You're claiming Peterson's cash was not the seed money for your financial empire?"

"I come from what is often called 'old money,' and I was wealthy long before the person known as Simon Peterson came into my life."

"What about the profits from Peterson's books?"

"Every penny of profit our publishing house has earned from the sale of Peterson's books has been plowed back into the company to support the good works of others. It was a way for me to attempt to mitigate the damage we had caused." Goodman's eyes locked on Sunny. "It is no accident or coincidence that I selected the name Atonement Press."

"Again, too clever by half. Did the same PR firm you used to create MAJIC Inc. help you come up with that name?" Sunny asked.

Goodman's eyes moved back and forth between Sunny and me. He had an unreadable poker face, and I didn't have a clue what he was thinking or where this conversation was heading. I did have a sneaky suspicion that if Sunny didn't modify her tone, I would soon be heading to the unemployment line.

Thankfully the limo rolled to a stop in front of our house before the inquisition went any further or got uglier.

I reached for the handle, but the door opened before I got there, and the driver offered his hand to help me out. I accepted the offer and stepped out of the oversized car. The arrival of Goodman's armada had created quite a stir on our street. Other than prom night, this may have been the only time there had ever been a limo idling at a curb in front of any of the houses. The Range Rover pulled in behind us, leaving no room for Cutter's Crown Vic, so he drove past us and took the next available spot further down the street.

Goodman's well-groomed staff of four hard men in dark suits clearly provided the muscle and logistics support while the two stunning female assistants in stiletto heels and tailored outfits provided the backbone of his mobile office. Just the sight of them standing on the sidewalk in front of our house brought the entire neighborhood to a grinding halt. Window shades went up, and people began wandering out onto their porches for a better look.

Sunny saw her coming before me, and she gave me a nudge.

Aunt Peggy, with a bag of dog poop in her hand, was walking her annoyingly yippy little mutt in our direction. Aunt Peggy saw Sunny and me exiting from the limo, and her eyes grew large. When Nathaniel Goodman joined us on the sidewalk, I thought for a moment the old biddy might have a stroke.

Sunny leaned into Goodman. "You want to score major points with the Maxwell sisters?"

"I'm listening," Goodman answered.

"Put your arm around Grace as you are walking into the house so that old lady with the dog can see you do it."

A puzzled expression covered Goodman's face until he noticed the rapidly building audience, and then his eyes locked on Peggy.

"Who is this woman?" Goodman asked.

"She is our aunt who knew Grace was illegitimate before she was even born, and she has been tormenting my sister her entire life because of it."

Goodman's eyes narrowed and his nostrils flared as he glared at Aunt Peggy. "I'll do better than that." Goodman whispered into one of his bodyguard's ear, then turned to me. He gently put his hand in the small of my back and guided me toward the front porch of our house. As we reached the steps, I heard Aunt Peggy's voice behind me, accompanied by the ear-splitting yap of her ankle biter.

"This is a public sidewalk!" Peggy shouted. "I will not go to the other side of the street."

Sunny staying two steps behind us so she wouldn't obstruct the view of any of the neighbors, softly said to Goodman, "Nice touch."

A wicked smile covered Goodman's face. "Anything for the daughter of Simon Peterson."

CHAPTER TWENTY-SEVEN

SAFELY INSIDE AND away from prying eyes, I slugged Sunny rapidly in the shoulder three times. "That was brilliant!" We both started giggling and quickly completely lost control of ourselves; we had to lean into each other to keep our balance.

Dad wandered out of the kitchen to see what all the commotion was about and pulled up short when he saw Sunny and me on the verge of needing a change of underwear from laughing so hard. His eyes looked past us and locked on our guest.

"Who are you?"

"Nathaniel Goodman."

Since he had intentionally kept himself out of the loop, the name meant nothing to Dad except that he was the guy we were picking up at the airport.

"Don Maxwell." Dad extended his hand, and Goodman accepted it. Goodman held the handshake a bit longer than necessary as he studied Don like he was trying to be sure he would never forget Dad's face.

"What the hell," Dad said as he saw and heard Aunt Peggy bellowing in protest on the sidewalk in front of the house. He wheeled in my direction. "I assume this is your doing?"

Sunny and I were in no state to answer. Dad shook his head and stormed out the front door. Sunny and I stepped out onto the front porch to watch the show, and a bemused Nathaniel Goodman joined us.

"I think this joke has gone on..." Sunny stopped me midsentence.

"Hold on, here comes Eddie," she said.

Apparently Aunt Peggy had called her eldest son to come defend her honor. Our overstuffed cousin looked like having to actually run a block and a half was going to give him that long-expected coronary. Meanwhile, most of the houses within earshot of Peggy – which, at the moment, was roughly a half-mile radius — had emptied, and the street had filled.

With his path blocked by not one but three of Goodman's well-armed and humorless bodyguards, Eddie's mind must have flashed back to the night before when he'd had the three-to-one advantage on his side and had still come up short. Now that the numbers were reversed, Eddie's face went from crimson to a dull gray, and all of his bravado melted away.

It was about to get worse.

"Do something, Eddie!" Peggy squealed.

Dad arrived and muscled his way between Goodman's bodyguards, grabbed Eddie by the front of his shirt, and bull-rushed him into the side of the Range Rover. Eddie hit the SUV with enough force it temporarily stunned him

"If you ever raise your hand to one of my daughters again, I will end you," Dad snarled. He pulled Eddie a foot away from the Range Rover again, then slammed him into it a second time. "You understand?"

Two of Goodman's bodyguards wrestled Dad away from Eddie, who slid slowly down the side of the SUV. For the second time in less than twenty-four hours, Eddie found his oversized butt on the pavement, stunned and dazed, and leaning against a car.

"Donald!" Aunt Peggy shrieked. "What are you doing?"

Dad wheeled on his sister. "Your son tried to hurt Sunny last night. If he ever does it again, I'll break him in half." Dad sloughed off the two bodyguards who were holding him back and took another step closer to his sister. "And my name is Don, not Donald."

Sunny gave Goodman a gentle elbow. "That's what real daddies do for their little girls."

I leaned into Goodman and whispered, "We've had enough fun."

He nodded and, in a voice that cracked like a whip, said, "Mr. Cutter." The private investigator's head snapped in Goodman's direction while the bodyguards kept their eyes fixed on Eddie and our dad. "Please extend my apologies for any inconvenience my unexpected arrival might have caused."

Cutter nodded and stepped aside, as did the other bodyguards.

Aunt Peggy, kneeling over her stunned son, shouted, "I have half a mind to call the police."

"Half a mind sounds like she's being generous with herself," I muttered, which brought another flicker of a smile to Goodman's face.

Peggy glared at Goodman. "I don't know who you think you are..."

Sunny stepped to the edge of the porch and shouted over Peggy. "His name is Nathaniel Goodman. Spelled G-o-o-d-m-a-n. He was a close friend to our mother." Sunny paused for maximum effect. "A VERY close friend." She paused again. "He's also one of the richest men in America."

Dad rejoined us on the porch, still full of piss and vinegar, and Sunny gave him a hug. "Thanks, Daddy," she said brightly. "Feel better now that you've got that out of your system?"

Dad gave Sunny a peck on the forehead. "Yeah, much better. I don't think Eddie is going to be bothering you again."

Sunny laughed. "After the last twenty-four hours, I wouldn't be surprised to see a for sale sign in front of his house tomorrow."

As we moved to return to the house, Goodman said to Sunny, "You realized you just implied that I was Grace's father."

"Did I?" Sunny said with wide-eyed innocence while putting her hands on her cheeks. "Huh. Imagine that." Sunny chuckled. "That certainly will give our aunt Peggy a thrill since Grace looks so much like you."

"What?" I glanced in the mirror by the front door then at Goodman; I certainly didn't see any resemblance.

"Same complexion. Same color hair," Sunny said as she eyed Goodman and me. "Up close, not so much; from a distance, maybe."

"Simon and I were sometimes mistaken for each other," Goodman said.

"From sixty feet away, my big sister could certainly pass herself off as your offspring. At least close enough to give Aunt Peggy a bad case of the vapors."

"Your mother's smart mouth and her wicked sense of humor," Goodman said with a chuckle. "That's a dangerous combination."

"Not so much when you're twenty-one and cute," Sunny answered with a laugh as she pointed to me. "It's a little tougher for the Princess of Darkness here to pull it off."

"This has all been very entertaining, but may I see the manuscript now?" Goodman asked politely.

"Sure," I answered as I motioned toward the side door. "We have it in Dad's gun safe in Mom's old workshop."

With the sun setting and darkness moving in, I flipped on the backyard lights. Goodman stopped abruptly when he saw the riot of metal my mom had created. "Your mother did beautiful work."

"Of course she did," Sunny said with a laugh. "She was a beautiful person."

Goodman pulled up short again as we approached the workshop, and a smile broke across his until-now stoic face as he read the words over the door.

Happiness Equals
Forgive, Forget and Release

"Elizabeth used to say that all the time," Goodman muttered softly.

For a brief moment, I thought I saw tears starting to form in the hard-nosed billionaire's eyes, but he quickly regained his composure, and they evaporated before they reached his cheek.

Don Maxwell flipped on the overhead lights in the workshop and strode purposely in the direction of his gun safe, which held the family arsenal of hunting rifles and handguns. He quickly worked the combination and opened the heavy door. Reaching inside, he pulled out the envelope containing the manuscript and placed it in front of Goodman on Mom's workbench.

Goodman studied the envelope for a moment, then, with slightly quivering hands, pulled out the manuscript. He immediately gasped. This time he could not control his emotions, and a single tear ran down his cheek. Gently, reverently, lovingly, he ran his hand across the title page.

"I never thought I would ever see this again," he said softly as he wiped the tear away.

"So, you think it's the real deal?" Sunny asked.

"I have never been more certain of anything in my life," Goodman said as he slowly flipped through the manuscript. When he saw my mom's handwritten comment on one of the pages, another tear ran down his cheek.

Goodman drew in air through his nose, then slowly released it through his mouth as he returned to his normal self. He turned in my direction. "Congratulations," he said softly.

"Why?" I asked.

"I am satisfied that you have proven your paternity, and I am further satisfied this is the long-lost manuscript Peterson wrote with Elizabeth Morris twenty-four years ago."

Sunny gave my arm a squeeze, but I was too numb to notice.

John Cutter handed Goodman his cell phone. "I have Mark Franklin on the line."

Goodman accepted the phone. "Mark, please begin negotiations for the publishing rights to *The True Path of Enlightenment*." Goodman's eyes locked on me. "Shortly you'll receive the paperwork from my legal department to begin the process of releasing all of the funds held in escrow by Atonement Press in the Peterson account to Ms. Grace Bliss Maxwell."

I shook my head. "No."

CHAPTER TWENTY-EIGHT

"Excuse me," Goodman said as he nearly dropped the cell phone. "Do you realize how much money is in that account?"

"It doesn't matter," I said firmly.

"You're refusing the money?" Goodman asked incredulously.

"Not at all," I answered. "Just the distribution." I pointed at Sunny. "One third." I pointed to Dad. "One third." Then I pointed to myself. "One third."

"That split would make perfect sense for the revenue from the publication of the manuscript, but you are the direct heir to Simon Peterson, and they are not," Goodman protested. "They have no legal claim to the funds held in his name by Atonement Press."

"Legal and moral are two very different animals, Mr. Goodman. It is my money, and I think that means I can distribute it in any manner I choose."

Nathaniel Goodman studied me for a full thirty seconds. I couldn't tell whether he was impressed with my generosity to my family or thought I was a complete idiot. From the expression on his face, I was betting on the latter.

"Are you absolutely sure?" Goodman asked.

"I have never been more certain of anything in my life," I answered.

"I don't want Peterson's money," Dad said flatly.

"Shut up, Dad," Sunny and I said in unison.

I put my arms around him and pulled him close and whispered in his ear, "It's not Peterson's money; it's my money. You've loved me and raised me as your own. As hard as I've been to deal with, believe me, you've earned every penny and then some."

Dad pulled away. "How much money are we talking here?"

Goodman spoke into the cellphone. "Mark, get me a current balance on the Peterson account." Goodman reached for one of Mom's sketch pads and pulled a solid gold pen out of his inside jacket pocket. "I'm ready," he said as he wrote the number down. When Dad saw the nine-digit number on the pad, he did a double take. He closed his eyes, shook his head, then looked at it again to be sure he had read it correctly.

"Fuck," Dad exclaimed.

Sunny and I both broke up laughing and started doing a happy dance. "Now we know," Sunny said.

A puzzled Nathaniel Goodman asked, "Know what?"

"In our entire lives we never heard Dad utter a cuss word," Sunny said. "Considering all of the nonsense Grace and I pulled while growing up, we had often speculated about what it would take to get him to drop the F-bomb." Sunny gave me a knuckle bump. "Now we know."

Goodman shook his head. "Interesting family dynamic you have here."

"Dad, Sunny," I said seriously. "Considering we now each have more money than we could spend in ten lifetimes, do you have any objection to all of the proceeds from the manuscript going to fund the Elizabeth Morris Maxwell Foundation?"

This was a day for firsts.

For the first time in my life, I saw Dad cry. Not just wet eyes — that happened from time to time. I mean real tears running down the cheeks, sobbing, crying. He grabbed me in a rib-crushing bear hug. "Your mother would be so proud of you."

"I'll take that as a yes," I said as I tried to pull away but Dad refused to let me go. "What about you?" I asked Sunny.

"I'm in, but only if I get to be the CEO of the foundation."

"Done and done," I said.

"Break clean," Sunny said as she pried me away from Dad. "We have something really important to talk about."

"What?"

"How fast we can we get the party of the century organized?"

Goodman cleared his throat. "It has been my experience it won't take long if money is no object." Goodman motioned in the direction of one of his female assistants, who glided up to us. "We want to have a celebratory party arranged for tomorrow night."

To her credit, the assistant didn't flinch or protest the short notice. Instead she simply asked, "Venue?"

"Right here!" Sunny said enthusiastically. "We're going to want a live band, an open bar with only top-shelf liquor, and killer food."

The assistant glanced in the direction of Goodman, whose head went up and down at most a quarter of an inch, before turning to me. "I will be willing to pick up the full cost of the party on one condition."

"Which is?" I asked.

"I get to keep the original manuscript of *The True Path of Enlightenment*."

I extended my hand. "You've got a deal, Mr. Goodman."

"Call me Nat," he said as he accepted my hand and tears welled up in his eyes again. "You and your sister are both so much like your mother, just in different ways." Goodman turned to his assistant, who was a bit thunderstruck by her boss having given some twenty-three-year-old kid he had just met permission to call him by his first name. "Have Pierre and his team flown in from New York."

"Will you come to the party, Mr. — ah, Nat?" I asked.

"I wouldn't miss it for the world." Nathaniel Goodman picked up the manuscript as gently as if it were a newborn and refused the offer from his assistant to carry it for him. Instead he clutched it to his chest. He turned to leave, and his entourage fell in step behind him.

I looked at the number Goodman — Nat — had written on the pad and shook my head. "We're going to need a really good accountant and tax attorney."

"William has a guy," Sunny stated, then motioned in the direction of John Cutter who was gloomily staring out a window into our backyard. "What's up with him?"

"Don't know."

Sunny and I headed in Cutter's direction, and he heard us coming and turned to face us. He looked as tired and beaten down as he had before his nap — maybe even worse.

"Congratulations," he said with a weak smile.

"We couldn't have done it without you," I said.

"What's wrong?" Sunny asked with concern in her voice.

"Don't get me wrong," Cutter said as he stared down at his feet. "I'm happy for you all, I really am. It's just…" His voice trailed off.

"Just what?" I asked gently.

"The last two days have been productive for you but just a cruel tease for me. While I've had some interesting new developments, I'm still Captain Ahab. I'm no closer to finding my White Whale than I was forty-eight hours ago."

CHAPTER TWENTY-NINE

SUNNY AND I exchanged looks. Cutter was absolutely right. We had gotten so swept up in the moment, we had completely taken our eye off of the ball.

"After everything that has happened," Cutter said, "I'll completely understand if you lose interest in the hunt for your biological father."

"It is not a question of losing interest, Mr. Cutter," I answered gently. "We're at an impasse. The pictures we got from Frank Taranto may be important, but frankly, I don't see how."

"Me either," Cutter admitted.

"We need that password," Sunny said. "Until we get that, we'll just be spinning our wheels."

"I know," Cutter answered as he bit off a yawn.

"You need some rest," Sunny added softly.

"Mr. Goodman's staff has booked me a room at the same hotel where he is staying."

On cue, one of Mr. Goodman's assistants approached us and addressed Cutter. "Mr. Goodman would like you to ride to the hotel with him in his car."

"Is it okay if I leave my car on the street?" Cutter asked.

"Sure," I said.

Cutter nodded and headed toward the house.

The assistant turned her attention to me as she looked around the workshop. "Would it be possible to use this building to organize your party?"

"Of course," I answered.

"We're going to want to put up a tent and install a dance floor…"

"We are?" Sunny asked.

"Yes," the assistant answered without a hint of emotion or stress in her voice.

"Outstanding!" Sunny said.

"Do we have your permission to move some of the art pieces?" she asked, then quickly added, "We will return them to the same spot after we're finished."

I looked at Sunny, and we both shrugged, then Sunny turned in the direction of our father, who appeared to be in a state of shock. He was leaning with both hands on Mom's workbench and staring at the number our new BFF Nat had written on the sketch pad with his mouth open in disbelief. "Hey, Daddy," Sunny shouted across the room. "Can Goodman's people move some of Mom's art to make more room for the party? They'll put it back after they're done."

"Sure," he answered absently. "Why not."

The assistant checked that off her list and moved to the next item. "Because Mr. Goodman will be in attendance, we will be providing security. We would like an invited guest list," the assistant said in her flat monotone.

"You've been away so long, let me handle that," Sunny offered.

"Thanks," I said, then started to chuckle. "You know who should be the first name on the list?"

"Absolutely," Sunny answered.

"Aunt Peggy," we said in unison.

After she stopped laughing, Sunny said, "All kidding aside, you need to release her and the rest of the Maxwell clan."

"What are you talking about?" I asked.

"The stars are aligning for you in a way most people on an enlightenment journey would envy."

"How so?"

"You are now financially secure for life, and you have no health issues casting a shadow over you to impede your personal growth. Plus, you've been making some real progress with your personal quest; it's time to move to the next level." Sunny grabbed both of my hands and stared deeply into my eyes. "Like what Mom always said, 'Forgive...'"

"'Forget and release,'" I finished for her.

"Exactly."

"Easier said than done. You didn't have to put up with all of Aunt Peggy's abuse your entire life."

"True, but this isn't about me, it is about you. There are two huge pluses to releasing her. First off, you'll both feel much better. Second, once you hold all the power in all your relationships, and no one can get into your head, life is an absolute blast."

"I know you're right, Sunny." I shook my head. "It's hard."

"No. It is not hard at all." Sunny shrugged. "Ask yourself this question. Now that you have all of this money, good health, and people like Dad and me on your seven..."

"Six."

"Whatever," Sunny said. "Why wouldn't you lance that annoying boil on your butt we call Aunt Peggy and get on with a happy and fulfilling life instead of letting her continue to make you miserable?"

"Fair point," I answered.

"Besides," Sunny answered with a concerned expression on her face. "You're in the danger zone."

"Danger zone?"

"You've suffered a personal loss in Mom dying, and you're just now starting to grasp how massive a loss it really is. That can trigger all kinds of negative reactions. You're vulnerable at the moment."

Before I could ask what lunacy Sunny was talking about this time, my phone chirped, and I fished it out of my pocket. The caller ID said *Atonement Press*. I hit the answer button, then speaker, but before I could even say "Hello," Mark Franklin started talking.

"I spoke to Mr. Goodman, and he told me we have a tentative agreement."

"Yes," I answered.

"Has the foundation you want to receive the revenue been set up yet?"

"No. Is that a problem?"

"Not at all," Franklin answered. "It will be a while before the book is actually in print; you'll have about six months before we make the first sale. You need to get a good accountant and tax attorney."

"We already figured that out," I answered.

"Sunny here, Mr. F. I assume most book contracts are boilerplates."

"Yes. Mr. Goodman wants me to fly into Cincinnati. I'll be there in the morning, and I'll bring the contract with me."

"Perfect. My sister has one hundred percent confidence in you. Don't try to screw her."

"Sunny," Franklin said softly, "this is the book I've been waiting my entire professional life to publish, and Mr. Goodman agrees. He has stipulated that all profit earned by Atonement Press for the sale of this book will also go directly to the Elizabeth Morris Maxwell Foundation as well as the royalties."

"Nice," Sunny answered.

"One thing," I said. "And it is a deal breaker."

There was a long pause before Franklin replied, "What is that?"

"My mother's name goes on the top line on the cover above S.A. Peterson."

Franklin laughed. "You scared me there for a second. Apparently you and Mr. Goodman are on the same page. He insisted on exactly the same thing. Anything else?"

"Nope," I answered.

"Good, I'll see you in the morning. Oh," Franklin added, "you both might want to turn off your cell phones and take your landline off the hook."

"Why?"

"With a book this big, we're going to need a distribution partner. That means I'll be calling a few of my friends. This is a pretty tight-knit industry, and when I tell them what we have, the buzz will start instantly."

Sunny laughed and turned to me. "Translation, Mr. Franklin here doesn't want us talking to any of his competitors before he has your signature on a contract."

Franklin chuckled. "I knew I liked you. But seriously, two days from now, maybe sooner if this makes the wire services, Grace will be overwhelmed. I'm going to bring Lori with me to be your PR liaison and gatekeeper."

"Really?" I said in disbelief.

"Fasten your seatbelt, Maxwell. In forty-eight hours, you are going to be the most sought-after interview in America. Everyone from national morning TV talk shows to the *New York Times Book Review* is going to want to sit down with the newly discovered daughter of Mr. MAJIC."

CHAPTER THIRTY

WITH EVERYONE OUT of the house except Sunny, Dad, and me, it felt like things were starting to return to normal. But considering what Mark Franklin had said and with our big party on the horizon, this was more likely just the lull before the storm. Whatever it was, the quiet and calm were well appreciated by everyone with the Maxwell surname. To avoid being seen by curious neighbors on the front porch, Sunny and I had taken up a defensive position on the back patio. The night air was cool and crisp enough that Sunny had bundled up in a sweater. For me, after six weeks in Jackson Hole, the temperature being still in the upper-sixties after sunset felt like a heat wave.

Sunny and I both had had enough wine in the past few days to last us for a while so we had moved on to large tumblers of plain water, no ice, with an oversized pitcher for refills sitting on the small table between us. Dad, exhausted both physically and emotionally, had called it a night early, so both Sunny and I were surprised to hear the sound of footsteps approaching. Turning, we saw William and Harrison headed in our direction.

"Hey!" Sunny said brightly to William. "I'm surprised to see you."

"Your phone was off, and I was a bit worried."

"Oh, so sweet," Sunny said as William fell heavily into the chair next to my sister. "With all that is happening, Grace's boss recommended we turn them off."

I smiled and nodded at Harrison, who in return gave me a playful grin. I motioned to the chair next to me, but he preferred to stand. I didn't know quite how to take that, but William, seeing our interplay, did.

"For Pete's sake, Harrison," William said with an exasperated tone in his voice. "No one is going to shoot me in Sunny's backyard. Sit down."

Harrison grinned at me again, brushed past me, and then sat down.

"My guys have made zero progress trying to crack your mother's password," William said.

"Figures," Sunny said absently.

"How so?" William asked.

"Mom has woven an elaborate game here, and she wants Grace to find the password and not have you hand it to her."

"Your mom was that clever?" William asked.

Sunny and I both giggled. "Oh yeah," Sunny answered.

"Without a doubt," I added.

"So," Sunny asked playfully, "is that the only reason you stopped by?"

"Well," William said innocently. "We did come over in the Mystery Machine."

"Mystery Machine?" I asked.

"It looks like the van from Scooby Doo." Sunny lowered her eyes and her voice. "But it has a few other secret uses."

"Eew!" I said with a disgusted look on my face.

Sunny completely ignored me, bounded to her feet, and pulled William out of his chair. "We'll be back in a little bit," Sunny said cheerfully. As Harrison started to his feet, Sunny pushed him back into his chair. "Sit. Stay."

William looked at Harrison, who said, "You officially have the rest of the night off."

Sunny made a silly face, first at Harrison and then at me. "Perfect! That'll give you two a chance to get to know each other better."

Harrison and I watched as Sunny and William disappeared around the corner of our house.

An awkward silence settled in over the backyard, and I had the distinct impression that, as laconic as Harrison appeared to be, if that was ever going to change, it would be up to me to get the ball rolling.

"How long have you been a bodyguard?" I asked tentatively.

"A couple of years," Harrison answered.

"Do you like the work?"

"Pretty boring actually," he answered.

"Really? Why?"

"There is a lot of downtime."

"I don't follow."

"Once I've got Mr. Hanson in a secure location, like his house or office, there isn't much for me to do."

"How do you fill your time?"

"Promise not to laugh?"

"Absolutely not!" I said with a chuckle.

"Then I'm not going to tell you."

"Okay, okay," I answered. "I promise."

Harrison eyed me with suspicion. "How can I be sure I can trust you?" he asked playfully.

"I make it a habit never to lie to a man with a gun clipped to his belt."

"Fair enough," Harrison said as he fished a Kindle out of his coat pocket. "I read a lot."

"Really!"

"You promised not to laugh."

"Unless you're into women's romance novels or vampire books, why in the world would I laugh at that?"

"Reading hurts my tough-guy mystique."

"Maybe for your Neanderthal peer group; for me it's a huge plus. What do you read?"

"I'm a huge fan of Golden Age hard-boiled mysteries."

Okay. That was a bit too pat.

"Really?" I said as I eyed Harrison with suspicion. Had William and Sunny, hoping to play Cupid, prepped him? "Let me see your Kindle." Harrison unlocked it for me then handed it over. Scrolling to his library, I had to admit I was impressed. My eyes locked on Dashiell Hammett's *The Thin Man*, and I thought it would be a good test for Harrison. "I always loved this book with Nick and Nora Charles. What was their dog's name again?'

"Asta," Harrison answered with a wry grin on his face.

"Right, right. And Nick Charles was the thin man."

"No," Harrison answered softly. "Because Dick Powell was so skinny when he played Nick in the movies, most people assumed he was the thin man. In the novel, the thin man was actually the murder victim whose body was discovered in clothes too large for him." Harrison's eyes twinkled as they locked on mine. "So, did I pass the test?"

"With flying colors," I answered.

"Why the game?"

"You telling me you like hard-boiled fiction is exactly the kind of thing my sister would tell you to say."

"Ahh," Harrison said with a wry smile. "Mr. Hanson really likes her."

"What's not to like?"

"Good point," Harrison answered.

"Do you have a first name?" I asked.

"Parris."

"Seriously?" I said as I tried unsuccessfully to bite off a laugh. "Like Paris Hilton?"

"No, like Parris Island with two *R*s."

"Parris Island?"

"Marine Corp training base in South Carolina."

"There has to be a story there," I said as I motioned for him to continue.

"My dad was career military and was stationed there when I was conceived."

"And?"

Harrison sighed. "My parents had been trying unsuccessfully for years to have kids and had pretty much given up. Then, surprise, surprise, right after my mom turned forty, she got pregnant with me. She insisted on naming me Parris after the place the miracle occurred."

"Interesting way to come up with a name," I said.

"I was just glad Dad wasn't stationed in Sioux City," Harrison said with a completely straight face.

It took me half a second to get the unexpected joke. I patted Harrison on the arm, which was as solid as a fence post. "Good one. Still, that had to be hard to live with growing up."

Harrison shrugged. "Not for me."

Again, I motioned for him to continue.

"Military brats move around a lot, and we didn't have time for social niceties and building long-term relationships. The pecking order was decided by who you could whip in a fight and who could whip you." Harrison shrugged again. "I was usually the biggest kid in my class and always the toughest, so my odd first name seldom came up more than once. Everybody has pretty much called me Harrison since kindergarten."

"So, you were always raised on military bases?"

"More or less."

I shook my head. "Small talk and chit-chat really aren't your thing, are they?"

Harrison shot me a smile that made my knees go weak but didn't answer.

"I assume you followed in your dad's footsteps."

"I enlisted when I turned eighteen. I put in my six years but decided not to re-up."

"Any particular reason?"

"I got tired of being shot."

"Shot?" I said with a startled expression on my face.

Harrison shrugged like it was no big deal. "Nothing serious, but after the second time I got nicked, I was concerned that three might be the charm and didn't want to push my luck."

"Did you start bodyguarding right after the military?"

"I took a year off first and traveled."

Harrison saw me running the numbers eighteen, six, one, and two in my head and instantly figured out what I was doing. "That makes me twenty-seven years old."

I felt my face darken slightly. There was clearly more to this beautiful hunk of masculinity than I had first suspected. The combination of being funny, smart, and able to see right through me, on top of being the physical alpha male, had me completely reeling. I had never met anyone like him before. All of my previous gentleman callers had been soft-handed academic types and not rough-hewn warriors who could slough off minor inconveniences like a few pesky bullet holes. I had a feeling I soon might be upgrading my love life from man-child to a real man.

Harrison seemed amused by the reaction he was having on me but made no effort to initiate any physical contact.

Please don't be gay.

"Come on," I said. "I want to show you something."

Harrison and I headed into the house and tiptoed up the stairs, so as to not disturb Dad. I wasn't sure what he expected, but after we arrived in my bedroom, I got the distinct impression, given the choice between seeing me naked or spending time with my books, I would have been a distant second.

"Wow," he said softly as he stood in front of my bookcase as if it were a religious shrine. "Wow," he repeated. He was so transfixed I wasn't sure whether he was even aware that I was still in the room. Standing next to him, feeling his body heat and raw physical power, I certainly knew he was still there.

Damn. Not only does he look good, he smells good too.

"You've got books I've never read that have been out of print for so long they're not even available on Amazon or eBay."

"When I was a teenager, while the other girls hung out at the mall, I spent most of my spare time at second-hand bookstores."

"I like smooth shiny girls, hard-boiled, and loaded with sin," Harrison said with a grin.

"Raymond Chandler," I answered. "*Farewell, My Lovely.*"

"You have quite the eclectic taste." Harrison's eyes lit up. "You a Hank Jansen fan?"

I waved my hand and made a face. "He was a bit over the top for my taste, and what are the odds a book titled *When Dames Get Tough* or *Death wore a Petticoat* could be published today?"

"No doubt," Harrison said as he continued to scan the shelves. "Could I borrow a few of these?"

"Help yourself," I answered as I put my hand on his shoulder and grabbed a copy of one of the few hardcover books off of the top shelf. "Here's the pick of the litter," I said as I handed him a first edition of *I, the Jury.*

I got exactly the response I was hoping for. Harrison's jaw dropped, and he caressed the cover. "Where did you get this?" he asked softly.

"I got it for twenty-five bucks about ten years ago."

"No way."

"An old used bookstore in downtown Cincinnati was closing, and they were practically giving stuff away just to get it off of their shelves."

Harrison put his arm around me and gave me a squeeze. "Where have you been all of my life?"

Back at ya.

Despite my desire to throw this amazing hunk of humanity on my bed and spend the next few weeks ravishing him until he was just a husk of his former self, I was able to remember that my dad was asleep less than twenty feet away. I was pretty sure Harrison and I were on the same page, but it seemed like he also knew this was neither the time nor the place.

After the moment passed, we spent the next few minutes going over some of my books and arguing over who was tougher, Sam Spade or Philip Marlow. We came to an agreement that we would both want Spade in a shootout and Marlow in a bar brawl.

Finally, I said, "We should probably get back downstairs." As I turned to leave, Harrison spun me around, and, as Archie Goodwin would say, he kissed me like he meant it. As soon as his lips met mine, I thought my knees were going to buckle. But again. This wasn't the time or the place.

"To be continued," Harrison said softly as he ran his strong hands up and down my back, making me shiver.

"There's a rollaway bed in my mom's workshop," I answered as I wrapped my arms around his neck and kissed him again.

I didn't have to say it twice. We dashed to the workshop like two overheated teenagers, and I was naked before Harrison even had the rollaway assembled. An hour later, I was pretty sure I had met the man of my dreams.

Coming out of the workshop, satisfied but disheveled, I ran into the last person I wanted seeing me slinking around in the middle of the night with a man.

And it wasn't my daddy.

"My, my," Sunny whispered, her face full of mischief. "What have you two been up to?"

CHAPTER THIRTY-ONE

I F DAD HAD caught me with Harrison he would have been disappointed in me, but considering I was a consenting adult and no longer his responsibility, I never would have heard another word about it. With Sunny being the witness, I had the suspicion my great grandkids would still be hearing the tale of how Great-Auntie Sunny walked in on me and Great-Grandpa Harrison. I also imagined, like a fine wine, the story would only improve with age.

William rolled his eyes and nodded first at Harrison, then toward the door. Next he gave Sunny a peck on the cheek. "I'll see you tomorrow," William said, then he and Harrison made their exit.

Damn. Harrison looks good from the front but spectacular from the back.

After the door closed, Sunny wheeled on me. "So?"

"So, what?"

"Did you do the deed or not?"

"Several times," I answered.

"And?" Sunny motioned for me to continue.

"Okay, okay. Harrison is everything your wicked little mind can imagine and then some. Easily the best sex I've ever had."

"Hopefully you shut the door and were far enough away Daddy and the neighbors didn't hear you screaming, 'oh baby, oh baby' at the top of your lungs."

"I'm not a screamer."

"Then you're not doing it right," Sunny said with a laugh as she tugged on my arm. "You can fill me in on all of the juicy details later. I want to talk to you for a second." Back on the patio, Sunny turned serious. "You've made amazing strides in the last few days; it may be time."

"Time for what?"

"You need to release Aunt Peggy."

"How do I do that?"

"Mom has a couple of Chapters in her book offering some step-by-step guidelines, which even a pigheaded nonbeliever like you could find helpful." Sunny made no effort to suppress her yawn. "I'm going to bed now. Do me a favor."

"What?"

"Leave your bedroom door open tonight."

"I never leave my door open."

"I know," Sunny said brightly. "But you need to tonight."

"Why?"

"There is a small chance, infinitesimal actually, you might need me later."

"Need you for what?"

"With any luck, you'll never find out."

"Find out what?"

"Just give me this one, okay?" Sunny said with a laugh. "Hopefully I'm just overreacting, but it costs you nothing and could prove to be invaluable."

"Good grief," I said with a snort.

"Can I take that as a yes?"

I nodded, then watched Sunny leaving. Since I figured we both were going to want to shower after our close encounters of the most pleasurable kind before bed, I gave her a head start on the bathroom. I sat back down in the chair I had used earlier, fished my phone out of my pocket, turned it on and pulled up the pdf of *True Path*. In Mom's introduction to releasing, she claimed there were basically two ways to perform this minor miracle. The first one was by making a conscious decision to let go of any unwanted feelings — release the emotion and it will release the power it has over you. The second way was to embrace the feeling and simply allow the emotions to become a part of you but not give it any power over you.

I was skeptical, but with the improvement I had experienced with Sunny's heart breathing, I was willing to give it a try.

Mom stated in fairly straightforward language that there were basically three questions I needed to answer before I could accomplish a release.

Question number one was, *Can I let this go?* When it came to Aunt Peggy, that one was easy. Hell yes. She was a second-tier relative, and, thanks to Sunny, I now saw I really didn't need to give a damn what the narrow-minded twit thought about me or my life.

Question number two was a bit tougher. *Would I let it go?* A lot of water had flowed under the bridge with Peggy and me through the years. There was a lot of hurt still in me. The primal desire — now that I was full grown and wealthy beyond my most fantastic dreams — to make her as miserable as she had made me was, frankly, tempting. Still, that would make me no better than her and serve no purpose for me or her.

The third question stopped me cold. *When will I let it go?* According to Mom, once the first two questions have been answered in the affirmative, the ball was now entirely in my court.

That was a good stopping point, plus, Sunny had enough of a head start and it was probably safe to head back inside. After I had finished showering, brushing, and putting on my PJs, I pulled myself under the covers.

As I repeated my relaxation exercise from the previous night, I had trouble focusing. The three questions kept intruding. Instead of the warmth I had felt the night before, an uncomfortable, foreboding darkness began to settle over me. Feeling a chill, I gave up and pulled my blanket to my chin, but it didn't help much. I rolled over on my side and tucked my knees up into a fetal position, but my body was quivering, and my heart was racing. I felt like I was on the verge of a panic attack. "Get a grip, Grace," I muttered as I pulled my blanket tighter around me. Closing my eyes, I tried to force myself to control my breathing, but it was a losing battle. Eventually, fatigue and emotional exhaustion won out, and I fell into a deep, fitful sleep.

CHAPTER THIRTY-TWO

I FELT AS IF *I were drowning. But I wasn't in water. Churning around me was a rapidly changing kaleidoscope of vividly remembered moments of my life. They spanned from when I was a little girl to things that had happened earlier today. Every slight, delivered or received; every unkind word, uttered or heard, was on display. Worse, everything I thought I knew and all my core beliefs were shattering. My entire life was collapsing into a black hole right before my eyes.*

Nothing makes sense anymore.

There is no purpose to anything.

Then a tidal wave of guilt swept over me.

How could I have been so cruel to my mother?

How could I have been so blind to all of the light around me and only focused on the darkness?

How could I have been so galactically stupid?

My eyes flew open as I felt a gentle touch. Sunny, either hearing me weeping or sensing my despair, had climbed into bed and spooned in behind me. She cradled me in her arms the way Mom used to do during thunderstorms when I was a little girl.

"Let it all out," she said softly, while stroking my hair.

"What is happening to me?" I asked as tears streamed down my cheeks.

"Shhh, shhh, shhh," Sunny said as she held me tighter. "It will be over soon. Breathe."

Feeling her warmth pressed against me, I slowly began to relax.

"I just had the worst nightmare," I said softly as I gave the arm Sunny had draped over me a squeeze.

"It was much more than a nightmare, Gracie," Sunny said.

"What do you mean?" I asked as I felt my heart rate returning to normal.

"You've been building up to this for days."

"Building up to what?"

"Did the nightmare throw every bad thing that has ever happened in your life right in your face?"

"How did you know that?"

"Do you now have lingering doubts about the entire framework you've built your life on?"

"I'm not sure I would describe it exactly that way, but basically yes."

"Good."

"How can a nightmare possibly be good?"

"It wasn't a nightmare, Gracie," Sunny said softly. "It's something much more powerful and spiritual. It's called the Dark Night of the Soul, which will allow you, if you want to, to awaken in a different reality instead of the one based on the concepts your mind has created."

"What do you mean, if I want to?"

"You're at a crossroad, Gracie," Sunny said as she snuggled in closer. "You can ignore this amazing gift you were just given and go back to the way you've always been. Or, if you're smart, you can take this opportunity to transform into a different state of consciousness. You're like one of those Joseph Campbell reluctant heroes when they have to face the ultimate challenge. You're Luke confronting Darth Vader. You're Gandalf on the bridge with the Balrog. It is time for you to shout to your old way of life, 'You shall not pass!'"

"Carpe diem," I whispered.

"Exactly," Sunny answered. "You've arrived at the moment where you can wipe the slate clean and start over."

"Are you talking about reaching enlightenment?"

"It goes by many names depending on your religious and cultural beliefs. State of grace. Born again. Nirvana. Satori."

"What do I need to do?" I asked meekly.

"Release all of the guilt and shame you're carrying around with you. Next, release the people, like Aunt Peggy, who still have power over you. Believe me, it will make you both feel much, much better."

"I'll try," I said softly. "Will you stay with me for a while?

"Sure. Anything for my favorite half-sister."

We both chuckled.

"But as soon as you fall back to sleep, I'm going to go back to my room."

"Why?"

"Remember the old hymn Mom used to always sing to us when we were little?"

While Sunny had brought it up earlier, I hadn't thought about that for years. Tears welled up in my eyes as I heard my mother's voice as clearly as if she were standing next to me.

You gotta walk that lonesome valley, and you gotta walk, walk it by yourself

Nobody else can walk it for you

You gotta walk, walk it by yourself.

Now it made perfect sense.

Wrapped in the secure warmth of Sunny's embrace, I instantly fell asleep.

CHAPTER THIRTY-THREE

I AWOKE WITH A start, and it took me a moment to orient myself. I was in my old bedroom, and the house was quiet and still. When I reached behind me, the spot where Sunny had been was no longer warm.

Rolling over on my back, I stared at the ceiling and tried to relax by controlling my breathing, but my mind was racing. I was ready to release every negative thing in my life, but I wasn't sure how.

I glanced toward my clock when I saw it.

The straw Mom had left me in her magic box was on my nightstand. Of course.

The little girl and the straw.

Amazing. My mother had been preparing me for this moment for my entire life.

Rolling back over on my side, I tucked my knees in tight.

Closing my eyes, I let my mind fall silent, and I visualized the spot in my chest that was the epicenter of all of my anger and angst. I saw the magic straw penetrating my chest.

In my mind's eye, I envisioned all of the hate and anger I had ever felt starting to flow out of the straw.

As the drip turned into a trickle, I saw the exodus of the faces of people from my life who had hurt me enough, sometimes years earlier, that they were still able to generate an emotional reaction on my part. I chuckled to myself as I suddenly realized how when you lived in the moment, the past was just an illusion. They were all just shadows tucked away in dark corners of my mind, waiting for the right moment to spring out at me when I least expected it.

As the trickle turned into a roaring flow, the straw grew to be the size of a water main that began to vibrate and emit an ethereal light. I saw

Aunt Peggy and the entire Maxwell clan being swept away, protesting and screaming. I knew their howls of protest meant the last vestiges of their power over me were slipping away.

No one has power over me now. No one.

As the flow turned into a torrent, my carefully crafted wall of self-doubt and guilt began to crumble. After the last brick was swept aside, the straw morphed into a shimmering sphere of golden light that fully encompassed me. Then, pulsating and getting brighter, the sphere began to grow and expand faster than the infinite speed of thought until, with me at the center, it embodied the entire universe and so, so much beyond.

Then it hit me. I had spent a lifetime making myself miserable when, like Mom and Sunny had always said, I was making this whole happiness thing way too hard. They were right; I'd always had the answers right at my fingertips.

Happiness Equals Forgive, Forget, and Release.

With tears streaming down my cheeks, I began to laugh.

Suddenly, I felt the warmth of Sunny behind me again, but I couldn't stop laughing.

Sunny held me tightly. "The universe has a wicked sense of humor, doesn't she?"

Emotionally drained, but safe in the warm embrace of my sister, I fell into a deep, dreamless sleep.

CHAPTER THIRTY-FOUR

WHILE MY BLACKOUT curtains will keep out light, they don't do much for noise, and I was awakened by the sound of voices in the backyard. Rolling over, I first noticed that Sunny had skedaddled again. Next, I looked at the clock on my nightstand and couldn't believe it. It was already past nine. I never would have thought it possible to ever sleep that soundly and peacefully twice in the same week. Maybe Sunny was on to something. I felt different. Lighter somehow. There seemed to be an absence of second-guessing and lingering doubts.

I threw the curtains open and had to turn away from the bright sunlight and give my eyes a few seconds to adjust. Turning back before I should, I squinted and shielded my eyes. There was a small army of workmen in the backyard. Some were busy moving Mom's art; others were in the process of erecting a large white tent.

Considering how different I felt, I was surprised when I glanced in the mirror that I didn't look any different. I was expecting radiance or something; instead I was still a complete mess. While much in my life had changed overnight, old habits die hard. My need for coffee first thing in the morning was still there. In fact, at the moment, it trumped all else, including primping and preening. I stumbled downstairs in a quest for caffeine and stopped in the doorway to the kitchen when I saw Sunny and Aunt Peggy sitting shoulder to shoulder at the kitchen table drafting a guest list.

Between my sister and my aunt was a plate with Sunny's absolute favorite thing in the world: Peggy's amazing pineapple upside down cake. Since there were several slices missing, clearly Aunt Peggy's apology for her son's loutish behavior had been both given and accepted.

Happiness Equals Forgive, Forget, and Release.

Then, I saw the last person on Earth I wanted to see.

Harrison, next to William, was leaning against the sink with a coffee mug in his hand. He nodded his head in my direction and seemed amused by my tousled appearance.

I closed my eyes and shook my head as I mentally kicked myself for not at least running a brush through my hair or over my teeth. Then I realized this could actually be a time-saving blessing. I figured if Harrison, seeing me at my absolute worst, didn't run away screaming, there was hope for a long-term relationship.

"Hey, Sleeping Beauty," Sunny said with a laugh. "I like the disheveled look."

"Thanks," I answered as I headed toward the coffeemaker, but Harrison, of course, was parked in front of it. We both moved in the same direction twice, trying to get out of each other's way. "Stand still," I said gruffly, avoiding eye contact. Harrison nodded and grinned as I maneuvered around him in search of my mug. I found it — where else? — in Harrison's hand.

I grabbed one of the smaller china cups out of the cupboard that held well below my usual minimum recommended daily allowance for a first cup of coffee and filled it as full as I dared. I really didn't want to spill coffee on the alluring pajama top I'd worn for the last three nights in a row without benefit of laundering and spoil the look.

I weaved my way back out of the kitchen and headed straight for the bathroom. A quick shower and the coffee worked their magic, and I was already feeling much better. I glanced in the mirror and didn't look much better, but at least I felt confident that I had regained the ability to communicate in sentences longer than two words.

Let's try this again.

With fresh clothes and basic personal hygiene tended to, I started back down the stairs. I had made short enough work out of my grooming that William and Harrison were still leaning against the sink, and Sunny and Peggy were still going over the guest list at the kitchen table. Sunny, seeing me coming, made big eyes at me, then nodded in Peggy's direction.

What the hell.

I walked over and gently patted Aunt Peggy on the shoulder. Since she wasn't expecting it and it was so out of character for me, it gave her a bit of a start. "I'm sorry about what happened yesterday."

"So am I, dear," she said hesitantly as if she were expecting another shoe to drop. "This has been a tough few days for all of us."

Sunny made big eyes at me again.

"What do you say that we put our past differences behind us and start fresh?"

"I would like that very much," Aunt Peggy answered.

Sunny gave me the eyes again.

"Come here, you," I said as I pulled Aunt Peggy to her feet and gave her a big hug. "All forgiven and forgotten on both sides?" I asked.

"A new day," Aunt Peggy said as she patted me on the back. "A new day."

Dad took that exact moment to open the outside kitchen door and started to come in. The sight of Aunt Peggy and me embracing caused him to stop so abruptly that Mark Franklin, who was a few steps behind, walked into his back. Dad quickly regained his composure and entered the kitchen.

"Someone's here to see you," Dad said as he let Franklin pass him. Then, since he still didn't want to be involved in any of this, he turned to leave.

"Please stay for a moment, Mr. Maxwell," Franklin said as he placed his briefcase on the counter and flipped it open. "I have a matter to attend to that requires you and both of your daughters."

That got Aunt Peggy's attention.

Franklin looked first at William and Harrison, then at Aunt Peggy. "A personal matter."

William nodded at Harrison, and they made their exit.

Peggy started to turn to leave as well, but I pulled her back. "This is my aunt Peggy and there is nothing you can say that she can't hear."

Sunny, behind Peggy, gave me a thumbs up.

Dad's jaw dropped again, and he headed to get another cup of coffee since he was now convinced he clearly was not completely awake yet and was dreaming.

Mark Franklin just shrugged and pulled out three number ten envelopes, the kind with little glassine windows used to mail checks, and handed one to Sunny, one to Dad, and the last to me.

"What's this?" I asked.

"Mr. Goodman was concerned that you might have expenses setting up your mother's foundation and he didn't want it to place a financial burden on you." Franklin nodded at the envelopes. "I realize this is only a small percentage of the total you'll be receiving, but Mr. Goodman thought it would be enough to tide you over until the final settlement has worked its way through the lawyers. If you need an additional disbursement, just let me know and we'll arrange it for you."

We all opened our envelopes, and inside of each one was a certified cashier's check for $1 million dollars.

Dad looked like he didn't believe it was real. Sunny looked like she had been expecting it. And all I could do was just gawk at my check.

"I have the draft of the book contract," Franklin said as he pulled it out of his briefcase and offered it to me. Without taking my eyes off of the check, I pointed toward Sunny. My wicked kid sister grinned up at me. As she reached for the contract, she casually placed her check on the kitchen table, directly in front of Aunt Peggy.

The look on Peggy's face was priceless.

I bit my tongue to keep from laughing, then turned my attention back to Franklin. "I thought you were bringing Lori with you."

"I did. She's out coordinating with Mr. Goodman's people."

On cue, Lori Donnelly popped her head into the kitchen. "They want to know if you've finalized the guest list."

Lori, while from somewhere in Oregon, always reminded me of every French woman I had ever met. She was an attractive, skinny-legged brunette who never smiled and always seemed to have a cell phone in one hand and cigarette in the other. Since she was not allowed to smoke in our office, she spent the bulk of her day outside by the back door, on the phone and smoking. I couldn't wait to see how she conducted business in the winter when there was a couple of feet of snow on the ground and it was twenty below in Jackson Hole.

I didn't think much of her. She treated me like the new girl and once even asked me to fetch her coffee. But, she had proven her worth to Mark Franklin many times over and that was good enough for me.

"Aunt Peggy," I said sincerely, "would you please do me a great favor?"

"What, dear?" she said with just a hint of suspicion in her voice.

"Would you please be in charge of the guest list for us? It would mean a lot to me."

Aunt Peggy's eyes lit up. Making her the gatekeeper and giving her the power to approve or veto who would be invited to our party was like manna from heaven to her. Peggy gathered up the list she and Sunny had been working on and turned to me. "Is there anyone you specifically want or don't want invited?"

I gave Peggy's arm a squeeze. "I have absolute confidence in you."

Peggy marched out the door with her head held high.

As soon as she was out of earshot, Sunny started laughing. "Brilliant! I thought she was going to have an orgasm."

"I have to admit, that was fun," I said.

"I told you," Sunny said. "The universe has a wicked sense of humor. For example, could us getting those checks have been any better timed?" Sunny's face turned gloomy. "On the downside, it means every one of our odious cousins will be at the party tonight."

"Target-rich environment," I said.

"That's the spirit!" Sunny said as she gave me a high five.

"I wonder whether she'll have the nerve to invite Eddie."

"Absolutely," Sunny said with a laugh. "While you were sleeping in, he came over and groveled to Dad and me for like ten minutes." Sunny laughed. "I thought he was going to wet his pants when he walked in and saw Harrison."

"I bet."

"Congratulations, by the way."

"I can't believe that with how different I feel that I don't look any different."

"It's weird how nobody notices, isn't it?" Sunny added.

Sunny and I were so engrossed in my successful release of Aunt Peggy from my life, we had forgotten Dad and Mark Franklin were still in the room with us. Dad's voice broke the moment.

"Do I want to know what's going on here?" he asked.

"Not really," Sunny answered with a chuckle.

Dad held up his check. "Is this for real?" he asked Mark Franklin.

"Very real, Mr. Maxwell."

After speed-reading it, Sunny slid the contract and ballpoint pen in front of me for my signature. "Initial each page, then sign the last one."

"Why the initials?"

"It shows you read the page."

"But I didn't."

"But I did," Sunny said.

That works for me.

I finished signing and initialing, and passed the contract back to Franklin.

"Do you need my big sister for anything else?" Franklin shook his head. "Excellent!" Sunny tore two paper towels off of the roll, cut us each an oversized slice of Aunt Peggy's upside-down cake, handed one to me, then hooked my arm and started tugging me toward the door.

"Where are we going?" I asked.

Sunny picked up her check as we went by and smiled. "We're going to deposit these bad boys in the bank and then do a little conspicuous consumption to get us ready for our big party."

As we headed out toward Sunny's battered old beater, I saw Harrison and William in a conference with some of Goodman's people and Lori Donnelly.

Lori was giving Harrison the eye.

CHAPTER THIRTY-FIVE

O NE HUNDRED THOUSAND dollars, in hundred-dollar bills, makes a stack 4.3 inches high. The stack gets considerably smaller after visiting a Chevrolet dealership and driving out in a brand-new, torch red Corvette convertible.

As Sunny and I were cruising down Beechmont Avenue with the top down, you could almost smell the testosterone level in Anderson Township starting to rise. With her long flowing blonde hair blowing in the breeze, every guy from nine to ninety was checking us out.

"So how was your first evening with Harrison?" Sunny asked coyly, confident she already knew the answer to her question.

"Amazing."

"Define amazing."

"I would say toes curled, legs quivering, eyes rolled up in the back of my head, never wanting it to stop, can't wait to do it again amazing."

Sunny gave me a knuckle bump. "It'll be even better tonight."

"Why?"

"After a huge release like you've done, everything is better."

"If it gets any better, I may want to buy a portable defibrillator because I think that man could give me a heart attack."

"Needing to have a fully charged defibrillator standing by adds a whole new meaning to safe sex, doesn't it?" Sunny said with a laugh. "I'm jealous."

"Trouble in paradise?" I asked.

"No, it's just…" Sunny hesitated.

"Just what?" I insisted.

Sunny sighed. "William likes role playing."

"Is that bad?"

"No, not really."

"What's the problem?"

"William likes me to dress up as a female Star Trek officer called 'Seven of Nine' while he has this off-the-hook custom-made Borg outfit."

"Okay, I still don't see the problem."

Sunny hesitated, then said, in a low deep monotone, "We are the Borg, you will be inseminated. Resistance is futile —" Then reverting back to her normal voice, she continued, "— is only funny the first couple of times."

I laughed out loud. "You're the one who decided you wanted to date a geek."

"Tell me about it." Sunny sighed, again. "He wants me to go to Comic-Con with him."

"In full costume?"

"Of course."

"You about ready to kick him to the curb?"

"Not just yet, but we're getting close to decision time."

"Poor baby," I said as I admired the interior of the Corvette. "So, when did you become the material girl?" I asked Sunny, as she rolled to a stop and was first in the queue waiting for a traffic light to change.

"The moment Mr. Franklin handed me a check for a million dollars."

"How does this snazzy car square with your whole enlightenment thingy?"

"It squares perfectly. I didn't take a vow of poverty. If you relax the mind and body, the universe will provide you with everything you need. I figured I was given this money for a reason and I wouldn't want to offend the universe by not spending such a generous gift. Especially when I needed a new car so badly." Sunny giggled, and when the light changed, she laid about thirty feet of rubber.

Instead of letting my mind tell me how many ways what Sunny was doing was wrong, I held my hands high in the breeze above the windshield and laughed so hard tears were in my eyes. "Is this what your life is always like?" I shouted over the roar of the engine.

"Pretty much," Sunny answered as she let up on the gas and brought our cruising speed down enough to be only a misdemeanor speeding violation instead of being in the second-degree felony zone that would get you arrested, thrown in the back of a police car, and strip-searched at the station.

"Why does all of this come so natural for you and so hard for me?" I asked.

"You're a 'process' person, and I'm an 'end-product' person," Sunny answered brightly.

"What the hell does that mean?" I demanded.

"A process person, like you, focuses on doing things the right way and in the right sequence," Sunny answered with a laugh. "An end-product person, like me and Mom, only focuses on the final result and could care less how they get there." Sunny patted me on the knee. "You wanted rules and a step-by-step instruction manual to follow. The problem is, there is no instruction manual. Plus, a lot of the stuff about a quest like yours simply cannot be explained logically, and you just have to go with it. That's a lot easier for final-result people to deal with than it is for process people."

"Interesting," I said.

"I realized early on there is no right way or wrong way to do this. Mom knew that too. She always gave us room to find our own way, which meant she drove you absolutely batty. That's also why living in our house was hell for you and heaven for me." Sunny glanced in my direction. "Did you ever wonder why I didn't go away to college like you?"

"Never really thought about it," I answered honestly.

"I knew in my heart-of-hearts that I wanted to spend as much time around Mom as possible. She gave me unconditional love. And, unlike you, I didn't have to go looking for my personal touchstone; I had already found it."

"Wow," I answered. "What about you going away to Yale?"

"Mom, knowing the end was near, insisted it was time I spread my wings and see the world."

"That sounds like Mom," I answered. "How have you been able to keep such a positive attitude through all of this?"

"I'm just grateful for all the time I had with Mom." Sunny gave me a furtive glance. "The better question might be, why are you so pessimistic?"

"What do you mean?"

"Have you ever gone hungry?" Sunny asked.

"Excluding when I was dieting?" I replied.

"Seriously," Sunny said. "A good chunk of the world — including us, for sure — has better food, medical care, travel opportunities, and a greater life expectancy than royalty had only a hundred years ago. In the history of mankind, starvation was common. Now some of our biggest health problems have become the side effects of obesity."

"Have you ever watched the news?" I asked.

"Oh, you mean that drivel on cable where people spend the entire day yelling at each other with the goal to turn everything big or small into a crisis that demands immediate action so they can get more advertising dollars or political donations?"

"That doesn't mean the world isn't a dangerous place," I replied.

"Always has been; always will be," Sunny answered while keeping her eyes firmly on the road. "I'm frankly baffled as to why so many people are always depressed or angry these days. I suspect it's from being bombarded 24/7 with negativity from TV, movies, cable, and the internet that is relentless and overwhelming — most people can't allow it to flow through them and ignore it. They have gotten so jaded they can't see all of the glorious abundance and goodness surrounding them. Sure, there are bad people in the world, but that doesn't mean they have to be a part of your world, nor do you have to be like them."

"Live in this perfect moment?"

"That's the spirit."

"How do you deal with the day-to-day interaction with people trying to manipulate you?"

"There is a reason that the stereotype of the guru, living alone at the top of a mountain, rings true. People are amazingly annoying to be around sometimes. I embrace humanity's lunacy and find it hilarious. Keep going the way you've been going the past few days, and sooner than you think, you'll get there too." Sunny gave my knee another pat. "I just wish Mom had been here to see you emerging from your chrysalis like this."

"Me too."

***

The trunk of the Corvette and the backseat proved too small for all of our packages, so Sunny rented an Uber to follow us home. It took some work, but I persuaded Sunny to put the top up for the ride back to the house in order not to muss our new coiffures before we had time to show them off at the party.

The sun was setting as we weaved down our street, which was lined with trucks and catering vans. There were also three vans with the logos of local TV stations and smiling pictures on the side of their perfectly balanced, at least in terms of gender and race, news team. On the sidewalk in front of our house, there was a knot of reporters and camera men. There was so much activity on our normally quiet street, several neighbors had abandoned TV and the internet and had put lawn chairs out in their front yards to watch all of the goings-on.

"Looks like the press heard Goodman is in town," Sunny said as she maneuvered her new 'Vette through the crowd into the driveway and turned off the ignition.

Next to the driveway, our neighbor, Mr. Henderson, was watering — overwatering, actually so he didn't miss anything — his mums. "Sweet wheels, Sunny," he said.

"If you ever want to borrow it, let me know," Sunny said brightly.

"You clean up good, Gracie," he added as he admired my new outfit and 'do.

"Thanks, Mr. Henderson. You coming to the party?"

"Wouldn't miss it. Should I bring my Skyline dip?"

"Naw," Sunny answered as she popped the trunk. "We got the food covered. Just bring Mrs. H. and your dancing shoes."

"Will do," Mr. Henderson answered.

Sunny gave the Uber driver a hundred-dollar bill for a tip for a $28 ride. He was so grateful he offered to help us carry our stuff inside.

Sunny waved at William, who was on the porch with Harrison and Lori.

"I wonder why William's still here?" Sunny asked.

"Maybe he has a bottle of Andorian ale for you," I answered playfully.

Sunny shook her head. "I knew I shouldn't have told you about that."

Harrison glanced in my direction and then did a double take.

Take that, Lori Donnelly.

Harrison got William's permission to lend a hand and walked right past Sunny and relieved me of my burden. Sunny took notice. With Harrison's back to her, she licked her thumb, touched her butt, then shook her hand while mouthing "hot stuff."

I was really starting to appreciate why everyone loved Sunny. There was nothing the least bit phony about her. She lived completely in the moment, and she didn't let anyone or anything dampen her enthusiasm for life. There was no hidden agenda. She didn't try to manipulate anyone, and if anyone tried to get in her head, she just laughed at them. More often than not, right to their faces.

If that's the end result of enlightenment, then I hope somebody figures out how to package it and starts selling it on Amazon.

To my surprise, Sunny's and my arrival had roughly the same effect on the pool of reporters as chum in water would have on a school of sharks: a feeding frenzy.

Having never experienced the aggressive shouted questions of small-market reporters trying to punch their ticket to the big time, I was a bit startled.

"Grace! Grace!" a well-groomed reporter in a *Channel 9-WCPO* blazer said like we were old friends and motioned to the guy with the camera next to him to start shooting. "Is it true that S.A. Peterson is your biological father?"

When the rest of the reporters realized who I was, they all surged in my direction and began shouting questions. I wasn't sure whether to be flattered or terrified. I certainly didn't know how to react. Fortunately, Harrison did.

He stepped between me and the nearest approaching reporter who was about to start heading up our driveway. "Please stay on the sidewalk," Harrison said firmly to the surging pack of jackals. As he had done the night before in the bar, he casually let his jacket open, revealing the gun on his hip. It had the desired effect. The media posse saw it and immediately backed up.

I had never had a knight in shining armor come to my rescue before. Despite my feminist inclinations, I had to admit, I kind of liked it.

"Ms. Maxwell has no comments at this time," said Lori Donnelly, who had magically appeared at my side. "I'll have a prepared statement for you later."

"Who are you?" a reporter at the back of the scrum shouted.

"I'm Lori Donnelly, Ms. Maxwell's public relations contact." Lori reached into her pocket and produced a stack of her business cards and held them high enough all the reporters could see them. "If you behave yourselves," Donnelly said, "we'll make Ms. Maxwell available for local interviews. If you continue to act like jerks, you can watch her on the national news." That instantly worked. The shouted questions stopped, and all eyes were now on Lori instead of me. Lori made eye contact with Harrison and nodded toward the house, then, brilliantly, she began walking toward the street and away from me as she distributed her business card. The media followed her like she was the Pied Piper.

I felt Harrison's hand on my arm. "Let's go," he said softly as he guided me toward the house and away from the press.

Mark Franklin is right. She is good at her job.

On the porch, William's eyes were locked on the Corvette. "Nice ride," William said as he gave Sunny a peck on the cheek and held out his hand. Without a moment's hesitation, Sunny dropped her keys in his hand and headed inside to unpack.

Harrison was clearly torn between following his boss or helping me. I relieved him of his angst. "I can take it from here."

"Thanks." As he trotted away, he looked back over his shoulder and said, "You look great."

I nodded in the direction of Lori Donnelly. "Better than her?"

Harrison glanced at Lori and laughed. "Too many deal breakers."

"Such as?"

"Smokes too much, never smiles, and doesn't read fiction," Harrison answered with a silly grin that made my knees go weak. I felt my cheeks darken, and I shot Lori a furtive glance. If she sensed that we were talking about her, she didn't show it. She had her back to me and was deep in conversation with the gaggle of reporters.

Satisfied she had the press under control, Lori turned and spotted me. She held up one finger indicating I should wait for her. As she began to stride toward the porch, her cell phone began to ring, but she hit the ignore button. At the top of the steps, she sized me up from head to toe. "Good," she said. "That's one less thing to worry about."

"Excuse me?" I said.

"Wardrobe and hair are fine now. We need to get you a new head-and-shoulder shot…"

"Why?" I demanded.

Lori nodded in the direction of the pack of reporters. "You're about to go viral, my dear, and do you really want that crappy Facebook profile picture of you sipping a blue margarita being used by the media and then seen by millions and millions of people?"

Yikes!

"No."

"Didn't think so." Lori waved her iPhone in front of me. "I can take a stopgap shot until we can get you in a studio." Lori looked around and sighed. "We need a good background." She snapped her fingers. "I know the perfect place: in front of your mom's workshop."

As we headed around to the backyard, I barely recognized it. What had once been our lawn was now a massive white tent over tables with white linens. At the far end, a band was doing a sound check. On the two front corners, attractive women in white shirts and black bowties were setting up their bars.

"Holy crap," I said.

"As you can tell by your greeting, the word is starting to leak out about what's going on here. Strap yourself in," Lori said absently as her phone rang, "because it's only going to get worse. Fortunately, we're out in the boonies instead of New York or L.A., and the really aggressive press haven't gotten here yet." She read the caller ID and hit ignore again. "You probably should stay in the house for a little while."

"Why?"

"Mr. Goodman's security team is good, and they've rented some local law enforcement talent to bulk things up, but they're all traveling with him. As soon as they get here and set up a perimeter, you can move about freely in the tent area. In the meantime, if you go out front without me, you might start a riot. Have you ever done a live TV interview?"

"No."

"We're going to need to do some prep, but you're a smart girl, and you'll do fine."

"Do fine with what?"

"We're going to fly to New York in two days, and you're going to do *Good Morning America*."

"I am?"

"By this time tomorrow, unless S.A. Peterson comes out of hiding tonight, you'll be the most sought-after interview in America."

We arrived in front of the workshop, but there was a steady stream of workers and caterers going in and out. Lori put her two pinky fingers to her lips and emitted an ear-splitting whistle that stopped everyone in their tracks. "Listen up! I'm going to be using this doorway for a photo shoot for the next few minutes. No one is to come in or out." Lori grabbed a pair of workmen. Turning to the first one, she ordered, "You go inside and stop anyone from coming out." Turning to the second one, she continued, "You stop anybody from going in."

Finally, she turned back to me, placed me in front of the workshop, and started taking pictures. "Let's get a few with you under that sign." Lori pointed to the hand-painted sign on the wall.

> *Happiness Equals*
> *Forgive, Forget and Release*

Lori took a bunch of pictures, then said, "Now look up at the sign like it has special meaning to you."

I did as I was instructed. As my eyes locked on the sign, I was hit by a thunderbolt.

"I KNOW THE PASSWORD!!!"

CHAPTER THIRTY-SIX

S UNNY WAS IN the kitchen when I started shrieking, and she came flying out of the house like her hair was on fire.

I was still screaming my head off while dancing in a small circle with my arms raised in victory. "That's right! Who's your daddy? YEAH!! YEAH!!"

Sunny grabbed me and gave me a shake. "Are you okay?" she asked with a bemused smile on her face.

Tears were running down my cheeks and my breathing was coming in gulps as I said, "I found the password!"

Sunny, confused, asked softly, "Where?"

I pointed to Mom's sign.

Sunny's concern deepened. "Gracie, that's six words."

"No, it's not! It's four words and three special characters, exactly like William's instructions." I could see Sunny was still not tracking. I ran inside the workshop, and everyone had a terrified look on their face when they saw the madwoman enter. "I need pen and paper." No one moved. "Now!" I screamed. That did it. I didn't know where it came from, but I suddenly had a legal pad and pencil in my hands.

I wrote out the password.

Happiness = Forgive, Forget & Release

I turned the pad around and showed it to Sunny. She read it. First, she started shaking, then she grabbed me in a bear hug, and we started jumping up and down in each other's arms, screaming at the top of our lungs, "Oh my God! Oh my God!"

"What is wrong with you two?" our dad shouted as he joined us in front of the workshop.

Sunny and I took a moment to regain our composure.

"We found the password!"

"What password?" Dad demanded.

He has really managed to stay out of the loop!

"It's the password to Mom's cloud account," Sunny said softly.

"Does this have anything to do with you trying to find Peterson?"

"Yes," I answered meekly.

Dad snorted, shook his head, and headed back toward the house.

Sunny, seeing the baffled expression on the catering crew's faces, held up her hands, and said, "Sorry, sorry! We just got some very good news and overreacted." She motioned them away with her hands. "Shoo, shoo. Move along. Nothing to see here."

Sunny and I headed back to where Lori Donnelly was waiting. Apparently she had been in public relations long enough that this wasn't the first embarrassing public outburst by one of her clients. "What was that all about?" she asked calmly as she selected the best head-and-shoulder of me from the block she had taken, attached it to an email, and sent it off somewhere.

"Grace may have found the password to our mom's cloud account, which will tell us where to find the elusive Mr. MAJIC."

"Really?" Lori said as she dialed a number on her phone. "I'm going to need to bring in more staff."

"Why?" I asked.

"I'm guessing the only title that would be able to knock *The True Path of Enlightenment* out of the top spot of the New York Times bestseller list for the next couple of years would be *How I Tracked Down My Dad, S.A. Peterson*, written by his biological daughter."

"Let's not get too far ahead of ourselves," Sunny said. "We're not sure this is the password yet."

A thought hit me. "John Cutter."

Sunny snapped her fingers, then pointed to me. "You're right. We can't open that file without him."

"Where is he?" I asked.

"I'm right here," said the approaching voice of John Cutter. "I had just swung by to pick up my car to head home when I heard you two were having some kind of psychotic episode back here, and I wanted to see it for myself."

"Grace figured out the password," Sunny said.

That got John Cutter's complete and totally undivided attention.

Sunny pointed to the sign over the workshop door.

"That's six words," Cutter said with a hint of disappointment in his voice.

"That's what I said," Sunny said cheerfully.

Looking around, I found the pad I had dropped and showed it to Cutter. "Oh my God."

"I said that too!" Sunny added brightly.

"Where's your boyfriend?" Cutter asked breathlessly.

"He's taking my new car for a spin." Sunny pulled her cell phone out of her pocket, and I watched her hit the second number on her speed dial list, but she did it so quickly I couldn't see who was first.

"Out of curiosity, who is number one on your favorites list?"

"The LaRosa's Pizza delivery number," she answered without even the slightest bit of embarrassment or remorse. Sunny held up her index finger. "You need to get back here. Grace has figured out the password." Sunny disconnected the line and looked up at Cutter and me. "He's only about two minutes away."

William was actually closer than that, or he had really pushed the limits of Sunny's new car. Considering Harrison, the ultimate tough guy, looked like he had seen a ghost — possibly his own — I was guessing it was the latter. William was coming through the front door at about the same time we got to the kitchen. We rendezvoused in the hall and started toward Mom's office together.

"What was the password?" William asked.

I handed him the legal pad.

"That's brilliant," he said as he pulled himself up to Mom's MacBook and got us to her cloud account quicker than I would have thought possible. He clicked on the MAJIC folder and typed in the password. He was just about to hit the enter key when Sunny put a hand on

William's shoulder. He glanced up and followed Sunny's eyes to John Cutter, and he immediately understood.

You really have to love a guy who can keep up. Apparently Sunny does.

William rolled out of the way and motioned for Cutter to do the honors.

Cutter hesitated for a moment, then hit enter. The file immediately opened.

Yes!

William reclaimed the keyboard, and we all huddled around the screen. After scrolling quickly through everything in the file, Sunny pretty well summed up the mood of the room.

"Well, that really sucks."

CHAPTER THIRTY-SEVEN

THE MAJIC FILE only contained the photos we had already gotten from Frank Taranto.

John Cutter, stoic, unflappable John Cutter, looked as disappointed as I felt. Even Sunny had a rare frown on her face.

William, on the other hand, wasn't ready to throw in the towel just yet. He pulled up the terminal on my mom's Mac.

"What are you doing?" Sunny asked softly.

"Your mom was just like you, Sunny," William answered. "She pretended to be a techno-idiot, but she knew a lot more than she let on." William slapped the desktop, startling everyone else in the room. "I knew it. She had a hidden file in that folder." William typed a few more keystrokes, and a Word document titled *Grace* suddenly reappeared in the MAJIC folder. William queued it up, then extended the same courtesy to me he had given Cutter and rolled out of my way to allow me to hit the enter key.

"Do you want to read this in private?" Sunny asked softly as she rested a gentle hand on my shoulder.

"No," I answered. "We've all come this far together."

I hit the key.

> *Grace:*
> *Congratulations! I knew, if you truly wanted to, with the help of Sunny and William, you would figure all of this out.*
> *I know how much you love a good mystery. You now have everything I had that led me to finding your biological father.*
> *Yes, he is still alive. Yes, I've been in contact with him. No, he did not know I was pregnant with you.*
> *It would be simple for me to tell you who he really is and where to find him, but what's the fun in that?*

One final clue:

It's not what you look at that matters, it's what you see.
-Henry David Thoreau

Or in this case, what you DON'T see.
Peace Love & Joy Always,
Mom

Cutter shook his head and sighed. "What the hell does that clue mean?"

All eyes turned in my direction, but all I could do was shake my head. "I have no idea."

"On the upside," Sunny said, "Mom has now given us everything she had, and it was enough for her to find Mr. MAJIC. The four of us will figure it out."

While I appreciated Sunny's positive outlook, I wasn't feeling very confident I could solve this riddle. I had already spent hours looking for a pattern in the pictures but had found none. They were totally random backstage shots of Simon Peterson and a few solos of Nathaniel Goodman.

In the over seven hundred photos, what was I not seeing?

We all turned our heads toward the window when we heard the band starting to play, and through the hedges, we saw shadows of our guests starting to arrive.

There was a surge of activity, and Sunny walked over to the window. "Goodman and his entourage are here. We should probably get out there," she said.

"You go," I said as I continued to stare at the screen. "I'll be along in a few minutes."

As William got up to leave, Sunny gave him the big eyes. William grinned, then turned to Harrison. "With Goodman's security detail now here, are you comfortable that I'm safe?"

"Yes," Harrison answered with a puzzled expression on his face.

"Excellent," William said as he glanced at me. "Then why don't you take the rest of the night off."

Sunny, with a mischievous gleam in her eye, turned to Harrison. "After what happened out front earlier, could you possibly stay close to my big sister tonight?"

Harrison grinned at me and nodded. "I can't think of anything I'd rather do."

As Sunny walked by, she gave my shoulder a squeeze and whispered in my ear, "You owe me one, and I want all of the sordid details."

I looked up at Harrison, who had moved close enough that I could feel his body heat, and fought back the urge to fan myself. I had the feeling if John Cutter hadn't still been in the room, Harrison and I would have found something more interesting to do on the desk than review my mom's cloud account.

Speaking of Cutter, he put his MacBook on the desk next to Mom's and pulled a chair up next mine. He fired up the original file Taranto had given us. I shot him a puzzled look.

"Let's look at the files side by side and see if anything is different."

We had only been at this for a few minutes, and we were already looking for a scraper to use on the bottom of the barrel.

The pictures were all exactly the same and in exact the same order except for two. They were the best and clearest profile photos of first, one of Peterson, and then, one of Goodman.

That didn't help at all.

As I stared, frustrated, at the screen, I tried to roll the stiffness out of my neck. It didn't work. Then I felt Harrison's hands on my shoulders as he began to give me an amazing massage. He instinctively knew all of the right spots and exactly how much pressure to apply. His hands were unbelievably strong but also so, so gentle. I didn't know how to explain it, but with his hands on me, I'd never felt so safe in my entire life. I controlled my breathing. As my body started to relax, my mind followed.

Despite the swirl of activity just a few feet outside of Mom's office window, my world fell totally still and silent. My eyes unfocused, and I asked for guidance.

Help me see what is not there.

Then it hit me.

"It can't be that simple," I muttered as Harrison stepped away from me, not wanting to break my focus.

"What?" Cutter asked.

"In all of these pictures, what don't we see?"

Cutter shook his head.

"We don't see a single photograph of Simon Peterson and Nathaniel Goodman together at the same time."

While that got Cutter's attention, his old cop instincts immediately kicked in. "That could just be a coincidence," Cutter said.

"Yeah, maybe. But those first two pictures aren't."

I opened the first jpeg of Peterson and sent it over to my mom's printer. Then I did the same thing for the one of Goodman. Next I attached both images to a message and sent it to William.

I snatched both pictures off of the printer. "Let's go."

"Go where?" Cutter asked as he rose to his feet.

"We need to find William."

"Why?"

"To give us absolute proof we've harpooned Moby Dick."

CHAPTER THIRTY-EIGHT

OUR BACKYARD WAS like something out of a Hollywood movie: Japanese lanterns; trays of exotic appetizers; and flutes of champagne, in real crystal and not plastic, carried by beautiful young women and handsome young men. Our friends and family were lined up three deep at both of the open bars. Letting Aunt Peggy handle the invitation list had been a masterstroke. As expected, every member of the extended Maxwell family tree was in attendance, including a few second cousins I hadn't seen in years. Now that they no longer could generate an emotional response, it was oddly nice to see them. Plus, the relationship dynamics had completely changed, not just with the Maxwell clan but with the entire neighborhood.

Aunt Peggy had seen the checks Mark Franklin had given us and had also heard him say it was only a small down payment of more to come. I was willing to bet Aunt Peggy had spoken to everyone under the tent personally and regaled them with a recount of what she had witnessed...then humbly noted that I had asked her to take charge of the party. I had the feeling that at this point, if I asked Aunt Peggy to shed her clothes and streak across the dance floor, there were better than even odds that she would do it. I made a mental note to not mention that to Sunny.

Nathaniel Goodman was sitting at his own table, which had been carefully selected and laid out by his staff. It was in the front next to the dance floor, well away from the crush near the open bars and near the band but not near the speakers. The table was bracketed by four clones of Harrison in dark suits and obvious bulges under their left arm pits. While they were not exactly keeping other partygoers away from Nathaniel Goodman, they were certainly doing a good job of giving potential autograph seekers and people who would like to be photographed with Goodman second thoughts.

William was easy to spot. He was sitting in with the band with their usual keyboard player standing behind him watching in awe and taking mental notes as William played.

At first it looked like it was going to be tough to make the short trek to the back of the tent because everyone I passed wanted to offer me their condolences and their well wishes. As we worked our way slowly toward William, I could see Cutter was getting antsy, and so did Harrison. Harrison looked at me and I nodded. By now, nearly everyone in the tent had heard about Harrison's little dust-up with Cousin Eddie and Team Erectile Dysfunction, and no one appeared dumb enough, or drunk enough, to want to try Harrison on for size. All of Aunt Peggy's minions were giving him a wide berth. Sensing the mood, Harrison put a no-nonsense look on his face and nodded to Cutter.

"I'll take point," Harrison said as Cutter placed his hand on the small of my back and we followed behind in the wake Harrison was creating.

"Excuse us," Harrison said. "Coming through… Excuse us."

The party was just getting started so the dance floor was still empty. Once we got there, it was clear sailing. William, seeing us coming, motioned for the regular keyboard player to take back over and rose to his feet. Sunny, who had her back to us while watching William play, turned and, from the expression on my face, didn't need me to tell her I had found Mr. MAJIC.

Sunny bolted across the dance floor on a dead run and nearly knocked me off of my feet when she arrived with her arms wide open. "That's my big sister!"

Heads turned, and when they saw Sunny lifting me off the floor, a round of applause went up.

"Please, put me down," I whispered into her ear. "Everybody is watching."

"Oh, right," Sunny lowered me back to the floor, grabbed my hand, and whispered, "Follow my lead." Still holding my hand, in a loud clear voice, she said, "Ladies and gentlemen, I give you the fabulous Maxwell sisters!" A louder round of applause erupted as Sunny turned back to me and whispered, "Bow."

Still holding hands, we both performed elegant stage bows.

At the table just a few feet away, Nathaniel Goodman's eyes danced back and forth from Sunny to me.

"You still going to release me?" I whispered as we straightened back up.

"I did that days ago!" Sunny said with a laugh.

"What? Why?"

"I needed to get out of your way so you could solve Mom's puzzle." Sunny leaned in closer. "So is it Nathaniel Goodman?"

"How the hell did you figure out it was Goodman?" I demanded.

"It was either Mark Franklin or Nathaniel Goodman."

"How did you come up with that?"

"You getting hired by the publishing house that just happened to hold the rights to Peterson's books around the same time Mom had tracked Peterson down was a pretty big old red flag for me. When Mark Franklin called Mom 'Lizzie,' I almost fell over. But then when Franklin said Goodman was the one who insisted he should hire you — that, combined with the timing, moved Goodman to the top of my list."

"Boy, we really think differently," I said. "I heard all of that too, but I thought Mom had probably contacted Goodman while she was looking for Peterson and told him about me."

"Huh," Sunny said. "I didn't think of that."

"It made perfect sense to me that Goodman offered me a job."

"Why?"

"He has a track record of taking care of people damaged by Peterson."

"He does?" Sunny asked.

"Goodman told us he was the one who set up most of the exit strategy. First, every one of Peterson's employees got a six-month severance package. Next, John Cutter lost his job from the NYPD because of his association with the Peterson missing-person's case, and Goodman put him on, essentially, a lifetime retainer. He probably also felt Mark Franklin's career might have suffered, so he gave him free rein at his own small press."

"Interesting," Sunny said. "You're right, I hadn't considered the possibility that Cutter and Franklin might have been acts of contrition. Even with that, last night pretty much settled it for me."

"What happened last night?

"You saw the way Goodman reacted. Here was this cold-blooded capitalist reduced to a slobbering mess as soon as he touched the manuscript. He had a personal attachment to it that went way beyond just finding a missing friend's long-lost book."

"And you didn't think to mention this to me?"

Sunny laughed. "Of course I thought about it, but all I had was speculation and suspicion and no hard facts. Besides, Mom wanted you to unravel this mystery and not me." Sunny patted me on the arm. "Don't worry. If you were still stuck in a couple of days, I would have given you another nudge in Goodman's direction like I did on the porch earlier." Sunny nodded at William, who was huddled with Cutter. William had the pictures in his hand and was nodding his agreement. "What's William holding?"

"Pictures of Simon Peterson's and Nathaniel Goodman's ears."

"Nice!" Sunny said as she gave me a fist bump. "Mom had their profile pictures at the top of her file, and with William's ear recognition program, we now have legal proof or, at minimum, enough proof to have a judge compel Goodman to give us a DNA sample."

"I'm willing to bet Mom saw William use his ear program when he stopped over to fix her computer," I added. "That's why she was so keen to get every picture of Peterson she could get her hands on."

"Right. So how did she figure out it was Goodman she needed to compare to?"

"Remember her clue? 'It's what you don't see.' In all of the pictures, there wasn't a single photograph of Peterson and Goodman together. It was like the twist ending of a good mystery novel."

"Oh, that's good! I never would have figured that out." Sunny gave William a hip bump to get his attention. "So what's the verdict?"

"After a quick visual examination, I would say it is better than a ninety-five percent certainty of Peterson and Goodman being the same guy. I'll send these over to my guys and see whether we can improve on that number."

"I attached the jpegs to a message. Check your phone."

William turned on his phone. "Excellent. I didn't hear it over the music. I'll forward it over."

"How long will it take to get confirmation?" I asked.

"Ten minutes, fifteen at the most," William answered.

"Perfect," Sunny said as she motioned to one of the young ladies carrying champagne to come over. Sunny picked up a flute and handed it to me, then took one for herself. "We're going to do a toast in a few minutes," Sunny said to the lady with the tray. She nodded that she understood and quickly moved away. An instant later, so many bottles of champagne were being popped it sounded enough like gunfire that it made Harrison and Goodman's security detail nervous.

Sitting with Goodman were Mark Franklin, Lori Donnelly (ecstatic to be at the adults' table), and several members of Goodman's staff I hadn't seen before. The new arrivals all looked very senior and very serious. Sunny and I both wrapped an arm around each other's waist, glanced in the direction of Nathaniel Goodman, and waited until he noticed us. Then we smiled in his direction.

He knew we knew.

Goodman's expression never changed, but he reached into his front jacket pocket and pulled out a folded sheet of paper. He slid it across the table to one of his staffers, who read it and looked like she would have been less surprised if Dorothy's house had just fallen on her. The staffer grabbed three of the other staff members, and they all bolted toward Mom's workshop. We couldn't hear what Goodman said, but Lori Donnelly suddenly got up and joined the exodus.

"I'm willing to give three-to-one odds that's Mr. Nathaniel Goodman's damage control team he had flown in, just in case," I whispered to Sunny.

"No bet," Sunny said as she grabbed the microphone off the stand in front of the band.

"What are you doing?"

"I can forgive Goodman for not knowing he was your father, but he has been jerking you around since he found out." Sunny glared at Goodman. "The man lied right to my face when I asked him whether he knew where Peterson was."

200

I chuckled. "No, actually he didn't," I said.

"What do you mean?" Sunny demanded.

"He outsmarted you. He didn't answer the question you asked," I said. "Instead he said he was willing to swear he hadn't seen Peterson in twenty-four years, which was absolutely true. He never said he wasn't Peterson."

"Dammit," Sunny said. "You're right. Slippery bastard."

Sunny flipped the microphone on and tapped it twice to get everybody's attention. All eyes under the tent turned in our direction. Sunny winked at me as she put her hand over the microphone. "Let's have some fun with him." She took her hand off of the microphone and beamed at the crowd that was now focused on her. "Friends. Family." Sunny pointed her flute in Nathaniel Goodman's direction. "Honored guests." Goodman nodded.

"Before we get started, we'd like to give a shout-out to our amazing aunt Peggy! She has worked tirelessly to make all of this possible. Peggy, you give us joy and laughter, and Grace and I are truly blessed to have you in our lives. Give it up for Peggy Maxwell Tucker!"

A wave of applause ripped through the tent, and Aunt Peggy looked like she might explode.

Thankfully she didn't start to undress.

I leaned in and whispered, "Laying it on a little thick, aren't we?"

"That's how you get to be the favorite niece. Besides, it is all true. Since you released her, she has given us a lot to laugh at."

Sunny has a point.

Sunny turned back to her audience. "There is an old Chinese curse: 'May you live in interesting times.' The last few days have indeed been interesting for me. I lost a mother but, for the first time, truly gained a sister." There was another ripple of applause followed by laughter as Sunny, without looking my direction, punched me in the shoulder. "Tonight we are here to celebrate the life of our mom. You may not have heard this yet, but we are setting up the Elizabeth Morris Maxwell Foundation. As the recently named CEO of the foundation, I will have to give you all some sad news." Sunny paused for effect. "As my first official act, I've decided to move all of our mother's art from our yard to a museum." This brought, mostly from our neighbors, the biggest round of applause yet. Sunny motioned for silence. "I know you're all distraught." Laughter rippled through the room. "But don't panic. I will personally see to it that everyone in attendance tonight gets a free lifetime pass to visit them." More laughter.

"What about the color of the house?" Mr. Henderson shouted.

Sunny's eyes found Dad in the crowd and pointed at him. "That is completely up to Dad."

"Painters are coming next week," he shouted back from the rear of the tent.

The crowd exploded.

Sunny motioned for quiet again. "We all know our mother was, how to put it, an interesting woman. But above all, she was a loving mother." Sunny reached over and grabbed my hand, then pointed her flute in Dad's direction. "Devoted wife and a colossal pain in the buttocks." More laughter. Sunny held her flute high. "To a life well lived!"

"To a life well lived!" answered the crowd.

During the applause, I motioned over Harrison, who leaned in so I could whisper in his ear. "If any of Goodman's bodyguards start to head in my direction during my speech, I expect you to shoot them."

Harrison grinned. "What's in it for me?"

"A night you are never going to forget."

Harrison shrugged. "Roger that."

Sunny handed me the microphone. "Thank you, Sunny," I said, then as she turned away, I slapped her on the back of the head, which brought more laughter. "Before I start, I would like to thank Mr. Nathaniel Goodman, who is picking up the bar tab tonight." This brought the biggest round of applause of the night. "You may be wondering why. As you probably have all heard by now, my biological father is self-help author S.A. Peterson, and he and Mr. Goodman were close friends."

My eyes locked on Goodman.

"In fact," I said with a smile, "Mr. Goodman told me, and I quote, 'We're probably as close as two people can be.' I can assure you all, none of us, especially me, would be here tonight if not for him." I raised my glass. "Mr. Goodman."

"Mr. Goodman," the crowd answered.

A wry smile covered Goodman's face as he nodded but did not rise to his feet.

"But now I would like to turn serious for a moment. There is an old saying, 'A son is a son until he takes a wife, a daughter is a daughter all of her life'. There is more to being a father than you can imagine. It is a lifetime commitment." My eyes locked on Dad. "He's the man who holds you when you're scared. He tends to you when you are sick or injured. He will let you cry on his shoulder when your heart has been broken. He'll cut the crusts off of your sandwich. He will love you with all of his heart and soul and forgive your moods and slights." With tears streaming down my cheeks, I held my flute of champagne high. "To the finest man I've ever known. Don Maxwell. My daddy!"

I handed Sunny my flute, dashed across the dance floor, and threw my arms around Dad's neck. He was crying so hard, he was quivering. The applause was so loud I was concerned that the tent might lose its moorings and collapse. An instant later, Sunny joined us for a group hug.

"Okay, you two," Sunny said as she tugged us toward the dance floor. "Big finale."

The vocalist of the band took the microphone from Sunny and began singing the old wedding favorite, *Daddy's Little Girl*.

> *You're the end of the rainbow, my pot of gold,*
> *You're Daddy's little girl to have and hold.*
> *A precious gem is what you are,*
> *You're Mommy's bright and shining star.*
>
> *You're the spirit of Christmas, my star on the tree,*
> *You're the Easter bunny to Mommy and me.*
> *You're sugar, you're spice, you're everything nice,*
> *And you're Daddy's little girl.*

As Dad and I danced, there wasn't a dry eye in the house. Including Mr. Nathaniel Goodman's.

Half way through the song, Sunny dashed across the dance floor and pulled the startled Goodman out of his seat. She dragged him to the middle of the floor, then separated me from Dad and threw me into Goodman's arms. Next, Sunny took my place dancing with Daddy. In a loud clear voice, Sunny shouted, "Don't forget you've got more than one daughter here, buddy!" The crowd exploded again.

As the band started into the second half of *Daddy's Little Girl*, I found myself slow dancing with a biological father who I didn't even know existed three days ago.

"We need to talk," Goodman said softly.

"Ya think?" I answered.

CHAPTER THIRTY-NINE

"Give us the room," Goodman said to the staff and bodyguards who had followed us into the house and were hanging around the edges of the kitchen. As they were leaving, a breathless Sunny muscled her way past the exiting crowd and into the kitchen.

"Did I miss anything?" she asked.

Goodman looked at me with his normal poker face. "Do you want her to be a part of this conversation?"

"Absolutely," I answered.

"What about him?" Goodman asked as he nodded in Harrison's direction.

"Absolutely," I answered again.

"Very well," Goodman replied, then cleared his throat. "First, it was very classy of you to not reveal that I was Simon Peterson."

"The night is still young," Sunny said with a laugh.

Goodman briefly glanced at Sunny, then turned his attention back to me. "For the record. I was unaware that your mother was pregnant, and she never shared that information with me until four months ago."

"If you've known I existed for that long, why didn't you reach out to me?"

Goodman sighed. "I wanted to, but your mother insisted I not contact you. She could be quite persuasive."

I have to give him that one.

"Instead," Goodman continued, "she came up with the scenario that, much to my amazement, has just unfolded exactly the way she had predicted."

"Meaning?" I asked.

"Your mother knew she only had months to live. She was deeply concerned about how you would react to her passing, so she wanted to give you a mystery to solve to take your mind off her death. She said ever since you were a child, when things got too much for you, you would retreat to your mystery novels and find solace there."

Okay. I have to give him that one too.

"She was easily the most remarkable woman I've ever met." Goodman said. "She structured the problem so you would have to involve your sister in the hope that by working together, you would become closer."

Mission accomplished.

"She was furious with me when I hired you without her permission."

"Why did you do it?" I asked tersely.

"I wanted the opportunity to get to know you."

"Why?" I demanded.

Goodman sighed again. "After I disbanded the Peterson project, I threw myself into my work. I never married, and I never had any children. Discovering you existed was an amazing blessing for me."

"Really?" I said in disbelief.

Sunny put her hand on my arm. "What else would you call discovering late in life, when you thought you were fated to grow old alone, that you had a child, an heir, by the only woman you had ever truly loved? That's not a blessing, Gracie, that's a friggin' miracle."

Goodman looked at Sunny and shook his head. "You look so much like your mother, I thought I was seeing a ghost when I first saw you at the airport," he said as he wiped a tear from his eye and turned back to me. "The brief time I spent with your mother made me the man I am today."

"Which is what exactly?" I asked with maybe a bit less venom in my voice.

"Grace," Sunny said, "last year alone the Goodman Foundation gave away over $1 billion dollars worldwide for some of the best causes imaginable."

"I still know how to make money," Goodman added. "Your mother taught me the right way to spend it."

"What was the deal with the whole Peterson thing?"

"I was an ugly combination of young, rich, bored, and arrogant. I thought it would be fun to have a laugh at the self-help industry. After meeting your mother, I moved in a different direction; the same could not be said for my staff. When I got the detective report, my worst suspicions were confirmed. I had already started the process of having Peterson vanish before your mother discovered what I had done."

"If you loved my mom so much, why didn't you try to follow her and explain to her what had happened?"

"After what she had discovered that fateful night, I knew she never would have trusted me, much less loved me, again," Goodman answered sadly. "I knew I could never make her happy, and I loved her enough to let her go."

Sunny did something totally unexpected. She jumped up and gave Nathaniel Goodman a hug. "That is the saddest love story I've ever heard. You've spent the last quarter-century atoning for your youthful sins that cost you the love of your life. You poor, poor man. I promise you, someday Grace will forgive you."

Someday, maybe. Just not today.

"Give me a reason why I shouldn't tell the world you were Simon Peterson," I said roughly.

"You're a bit late for that," Goodman answered. "As your mother requested — insisted, actually — as soon as you figured out who I was, I would reveal my past myself. The press release went out about the time I entered this room."

EPILOGUE

A S SOON AS the news hit the wire service that Nathaniel Goodman was the long missing S.A. Peterson, my fifteen minutes of fame were officially up. I was the sidebar, the afterthought, the heartwarming human interest story that ran on page 4A. Nathaniel Goodman, one of the world's richest men, coming out as the mysterious Mr. MAJIC was front-page news worldwide. Cable news was already having one of their famous 24/7 wall-to-wall, "we have nothing new to say so we'll keep repeating ourselves over and over" marathons.

Sunny and I were sitting side by side, under the now nearly empty tent, well on our way to getting sloppy drunk. John Cutter, had quickly gotten over his anger with Goodman for stringing him along for over twenty years, Now, scotch in hand, he was chatting up Mark Franklin and had a smile on his face for the ages.

"What did you say to William?" Sunny asked.

"What do you mean?" I asked innocently.

Sunny gave me the big eyes.

"Okay, okay," I said. "I just told him if he wants his penis to continue to boldly go where few men had gone before, he might want to put his Borg outfit in the back of the closet."

"Thanks." Sunny clinked my glass.

"Did you cancel going to Comic-Con?"

"Oh, hell no," Sunny said with a laugh. "Do you know how good I look in that Seven of Nine outfit? Jeri Ryan has nothing on me." Sunny took another sip of scotch. "How did your private chat with Goodman go?"

"Much better than I expected. Speaking of Nat," I said, looking around, "where is he?

Sunny and I spotted him and Dad having a conversation just outside Mom's workshop.

"I'd love to be a fly on the wall," I said.

"Notice that one of Goodman's bodyguards is discreetly behind Dad but within range to stop him from punching Nat in the nose."

"You've been hanging around Harrison too much."

We both eyed the impressive hunk of manhood standing behind William, who was playing cover songs on the piano, as the rest of the band was packing up. Harrison had sensed I wanted some private time with my sister and had given us some space.

This one was a keeper.

Harrison felt my eyes on him and he smiled in my direction.

Sunny took another sip of sixty-year-old scotch and made a face. Neither Sunny nor I were scotch drinkers, but we felt obligated to at least try it since, according to Goodman, it was the best in the world. Despite costing over $1,000 an ounce, it still tasted like scotch to me.

"How exactly did you persuade William to give Harrison the night off?"

"I made it clear to William that I'm getting laid tonight," Sunny said. "And I informed him if he wants to be an active participant, he would have to be willing to make certain accommodations to your basest carnal needs."

"Best half-sister ever." I clinked Sunny's glass.

"So, what are you going to do?" Sunny asked.

"With Harrison?"

"No," Sunny answered as my response nearly caused her to choke on her scotch. "What are you going to do with the rest of your life?"

"I'm sure as hell not spending the winter in Wyoming," I answered. "I don't want to live anywhere they measure snow by the foot instead of the inch."

"So where are you going?"

I stuck my nose in the air and faked a socialite's nasal voice. "I'll be flying back to the city tomorrow on one of Daddy's jets."

"Are you just going to live a life of leisure?" Sunny asked with a chuckle.

"Nope," I said as I took another sip of scotch. "I've got a new job."

"Doing what?"

"A management training program."

"Management training?"

"Nat said he would like to start grooming me to eventually take over the reins of our company when he is ready to step down."

Sunny made a face. "When did it become 'our' company?"

"Evidently, shortly after I visited Mom for the last time."

"You lost me," Sunny asked.

"Apparently, our conniving mother took some of my hairs from my hairbrush and sent them to Nat." I sighed. "When he got confirmation of paternity, he made major changes to his financial holdings. As soon as we get back to Manhattan and I sign a few papers, I'll be the second-largest shareholder of Goodman International stock and the primary beneficiary of his will."

"Wow," Sunny answered. "Still, CEO of a major international corporation is a huge job."

"I know," I answered with a sigh. "I told him I don't see it ever happening."

"Was he disappointed?"

"No, not even a little bit." I said with a chuckle. "In fact, I think he was channeling his inner-mom. He said he would support whatever I wanted to do that would make me happy."

"Aww, that is so sweet. So, what do think would make you happy?"

"Taking over as publisher of Atonement Press."

Sunny laughed so hard she almost spilled her drink again. "Please let me be there when Goodman breaks the news to Mark Franklin."

"Done," I said as I clinked Sunny's glass again.

"What about Harrison?" she asked.

"I've invited him to come along with me."

"What did he say?"

"He's thinking about it."

"What if his male ego won't let him be a kept man?"

"If he can get past that, then I think we could be very good for each other. But he's a full-grown man, and I'm not going to try to force him to do anything he doesn't want to do just to please me," I answered.

"You've really figured this all out, haven't you?"

"A work in progress," I answered. "You still headed to Yale?"

Sunny made a face. "I'm already enrolled and will likely give it a semester. But with all of this money in my pocket, I'm already getting the itch."

"What kind of itch?" I asked.

"I've always wanted to travel."

"Really? How long are you thinking about knocking around?"

"Not more than fifty or sixty years."

"If you need a wing-woman for any of your adventures, let me know. In the meantime, it's less than ninety miles from New Haven to Midtown."

"Still a long train ride," Sunny said.

"But only a twenty-minute helicopter ride," I said

"You have a helicopter?"

"Apparently I have several, and Nat said I can have my own jet if I want one."

"Damn," Sunny said. "If you ever decide to write that book Lori suggested about tracking down Peterson, I have the perfect title."

"Why do I find that not the least bit surprising?"

"*Grace Has Two Daddies.*" Sunny paused and licked her lips, then continued, "*And they both spoil the hell out of her.*"

"Speaking of my two daddies." We turned our attention back to Dad and Goodman. "What do you think they're saying?"

"They both loved Mom and each had a child with her. That's a pretty good common ground to start on."

Suddenly, across the way, Dad's arms were flailing away, and Nathaniel Goodman was laughing so hard he had tears in his eyes.

"Mom story," we said in unison.

"I'm kind of starting to like Goodman," Sunny said.

"Yeah, me too."

Turning my attention back to the dance floor, I saw Harrison heading in my direction. He held a hand out to me. "May I have this dance?"

"You dance too?" I asked as I took his offered hand and rose to my feet.

"Not really," Harrison answered.

"Good," I said seductively. "I have a much better idea."

"I can't stay out too late," Harrison said with a grin.

"Why not?" I asked.

"I'm flying to New York in the morning."

AFTERWARD

Many of the concepts and techniques discussed in *What Ever Happened to Mr. MAJIC?* came from Dr. Jeffery A. Martin and the experiences of the thousands of people who have participated in his 12+ years of global scientific research into experiences like enlightenment, nonduality, persistent mystical experience, the peace that passeth understanding, unitive experience, God consciousness, and more.

For additional information about this research, visit:
NonSymbolic.org

For information on his project that helps people transition into the experience of life that Grace, Sunny, and their mom have, visit:
FindersCourse.com

RELATED BOOKS BY THE AUTHORS

By Rod Pennington and Dr. Jeffery A. Martin

The Fourth Awakening Series
The Fourth Awakening
The Gathering Darkness
The Fourth Awakening Chronicles I
The Fourth Awakening Chronicles II
The Fourth Awakening Chronicles III
The Fourth Awakening Chronicles IV

By Rod Pennington

Indweller

The "Family" Series
Family Reunion
Family Business
Family Secrets
Family Honor
Family Debt

By Dr. Jeffery A. Martin

The God Formula
The Complete Guide to Reiki
The Complete Guide to Reiki, Vol. II

8/19

CPSIA information can be obtained
at www.ICGtesting.com
Printed in the USA
LVHW041224280719
625632LV00013B/666

9 781572 421653